THE
OUTSIDE
SHOT

Walter Dean Myers

LAUREL-LEAF
BOOKS

Published by
Bantam Doubleday Dell Books for Young Readers
a division of
Bantam Doubleday Dell Publishing Group, Inc.
1540 Broadway
New York, New York 10036

This novel by Walter Dean Myers is based on an original screen treatment by John Ballard.

ISBN: 0-440-96784-8

RL: 4.7

Reprinted by arrangement with Delacorte Press

Printed in the United States of America

January 1987

20 19

OPM

1

"Hey Lonnie, what you doing round here? Thought you was supposed to be going off to some college?" Sister Boone, from the church my mother went to, was fanning herself as she sat on a wooden chair in front of one of the brownstones down the block from where I lived. She was fat, and she leaned her head back so the breeze from the fan would get at the fold in her neck.

"I got about an hour before I leave for the airport," I said.

"Well, you take care of yourself and keep your mind on Jesus," she said. "You hear me?"

"Yes, ma'am."

"What you doing, takin' you a last look around this old raggedy neighborhood?"

"Be a long time before I see it again," I said.

"You ain't missing much," she said, pulling her dress away from where the sweat made it stick to her leg. "Where 'bout you going?"

"Montclare State," I said, "that's in Indiana. It's a pretty small school."

"I don't care how small it is," she said, looking up the street. "Jesus out there same as he's here. You keep your mind on him and don't be doing nothing to shame yourself. Go on, now."

A junkie was nodding out on the corner. He saw me coming and tried to pull his manhood together until I passed, but couldn't quite get it together. Some guys were sitting in front of the bodega playing dominoes. A dog curled in a little knot under the table, with only his tail moving when the domino players slammed a piece down on the table. Everything had it's place. I never figured mine to be in no Indiana, though.

I had been playing ball most of my life, mostly because it was a thing I could do. Then a dude named Cal Jones had got me and some other guys from around the way in this tournament where a coach from Montclare saw me. He said I had a nice game even though I was a little rough around the edges. A week later I got a letter saying that if I graduated high school I could get a full scholarship. Everybody was running down how wonderful it was, and I guess it was, because it was what I had been hoping for. I was a little uptight about it, though, because I didn't know how I'd do in Indiana.

By the time I said my last good-byes to the people in my mother's apartment building and started for the airport I chilled out a little, but not much. My moms went with me to the airport and we went through one of them things about not knowing what to say to each other. She was boohooing and whatnot and it almost got to me but I caught myself.

"You go out there and play good and do what they tell you," she said.

Moms was okay. She didn't know boo about no basketball, but she was okay.

I had to change planes in Indianapolis and the plane I switched to was one of them little numbers that bounce around something terrible. I thought I was going to throw up a couple of times but the chick that sat next to me was so cool she calmed me down. Hitting the ground was on the money, just the same.

The letter from the school had said that someone would meet me at the airport. Time I got out of the bathroom and found my bags a short, stocky guy had come up to me and asked if I was Lonnie Jackson.

"Yeah," I said.

He shook my hand like maybe he didn't want to or something, told me his name was Clayton Leeds, and then told me to follow him to his car.

I wanted to talk to the guy, to start off on a friendly basis, but he acted as if he didn't want to talk so I didn't say much.

We got to the college and I was surprised. I had thought it would look something like City College in New York, just another building in a regular neighborhood, but it wasn't. It looked like one of those schools you see in the movies with lots of grass and ivy on the walls of the buildings. We passed some students, all white, before we stopped in front of a red brick building.

"This is Orly Hall, where you'll be staying," Leeds said. "It's the second floor, room two twenty. There's practice tomorrow morning at nine. You need anything tonight?"

I heard myself saying no and a moment later I was struggling up the stairs with my bags.

I found room two twenty and knocked on the door. I heard a voice, a loud noise as if someone had banged into something, then the door opened. The guy that opened it was blond and blue-eyed and about an inch or so taller than me. He was thin with wide shoulders and a broad neck that made you think he was bigger than he was.

"I'm Lonnie Jackson," I said. "I'm supposed to be staying in here."

"Oh, come in," he said, holding out his hand. "I'm Colin Young."

I shook his hand and then brought my bags in. It was a large room with four beds, two on one wall and two on the other. I could see a bathroom in one corner and, on the far wall, a small refrigerator. There were pennants all over the wall. Most of them were old and faded from years ago.

"You alone?" Colin asked. He had a funny accent, one I hadn't heard before.

"Yeah, a guy picked me up at the station—what's his name—"

"Leeds?" Colin asked.

"Leeds, yeah, that's it. He just dropped me off at the front steps."

"That's like him," Colin said. "He's the assistant coach. Where you from?"

"New York."

"I'm from a little town in Illinois called Cisne," Colin said. "I've got some Cokes in the fridge, why don't you grab a seat and relax."

"How long you been here?" I asked as Colin went to the refrigerator to get the Cokes. The refrigerator was so small he had to get on his knees to find them. He handed me one.

"Almost a week," he answered, popping his can. "I got here first, then Juice and Sly."

"Who?"

"Juice is from Gary, Indiana," Colin said. "Sly's from Detroit. They seem to be pretty nice guys. We're the only new guys here. Everybody else either played last year or they were redshirting."

"What's that?"

"Redshirting?" Colin sat on the bed and crossed his legs at the ankle. "Say they have four good guards, right?"

"Okay."

"And they're all in the same year. That means they all can't play on the first team and they'll all leave together and you won't have any new guards because you can't recruit a good new guard and sit him on the bench for three years. So they make one or two guys sit out the year so they have another year of eligibility left when the other guards graduate. They practice with the team and everything but they have to wear different uniforms because they're not officially with the team. They say most schools have them."

"That's new to me," I said.

"There are a lot of things here I never heard of," Colin said, shaking his head. "You eat anything?"

"Not since the airplane."

"We can go down later and get something from the coffee shop," Colin said. "It's open most of the night."

"You smell something burning?" I asked.

A thin wisp of smoke was coming up from the waste-paper basket. Colin ran over to it and dumped it on the floor. The paper went up in a blaze.

"What happened, man?" I took a step backwards.

"Oh, sweat, I got a fire started."

"I can see that."

Colin started trying to stamp out the fire, and I helped him. It took about two or three minutes to get the last of the smoldering paper extinguished.

"What you do—put a cigarette or something in there?" I asked.

"When I heard you knock on the door I thought that maybe Leeds was with you," Colin said. "I heard he was going to pick up another player today and, you know, we're not supposed to smoke during the school year."

I watched Colin try to get all the charred paper back into the basket. He went into the bathroom, wet a washcloth, and started wiping it up. I got another washcloth and gave the guy a hand.

"Appreciate it," Colin said. "I really do. You just breathe hard around here and Leeds is all over you."

"Oh, yeah? What kind of ball do they play?" I asked.

"I don't know." Colin said. He opened the window to let the room air out. "Leeds has this calculator and he adds up everything you do. You get a rebound, Leeds puts that down. You shoot, he puts that down, then he gives all the numbers to Coach Teufel and he figures them out on *his* calculator."

"Yeah, yeah, but how do they play ball?" I asked again. "They go for one on one, they go for outside shooting? You know what I mean?"

"Hey, I know what *you* mean, but I swear I don't know what kind of ball they play," Colin said. "All they talk about is, you have to have so many of each thing according to your position. Me, I'm playing forward, so I got to have six rebounds, five assists, two blocks, and ten points, every game. That's what the coach says."

"Well, that don't make much sense to me, man. We played a lot of one on one where I came from, but this guy I knew, he was saying that this kind of school don't play a lot of one on one."

"Maybe, maybe not," Colin said. "I played on this high school team over in Cisne and we just went out and did the best we could. Didn't do a whole lot of talking about how we were playing or anything. The ones that could shoot did that and everybody else did what they could do."

"I guess I'll find out," I said. "You seen any of these . . . what you call these cats? What kind of shirts they wear?"

"Redshirts."

"Yeah, you see any of them play?"

"Uh-huh. They're okay," Colin said. "I mean, they're not special or anything, but that's not what gets you when you're practicing."

"What you mean?"

"Everybody knows them and they don't know us," Colin said. "They know the plays and everything. The way I figure, they're checking us out the same way we're checking them out."

"You like it here?"

"Sure," Colin grinned. "It beats hanging around Cisne waiting for somebody to come along with a job. I'll tell you one thing, though. If I were looking for a place to play ball for fun, this place sure wouldn't be on the top of my list."

"That's the way it seems," I said. "Where do you put your clothes?"

"Juice and Sly share that dresser over there," Colin said, "and you and me can take this one. I have my stuff in the top two drawers."

"Okay."

"That closet over there is for all of us, it's big enough to walk around in. They take the right side—"

"And we got the left," I said.

"Most of the stuff ends up on the floor," Colin said. "Or we kick it under the bed to make the room look neater."

"Looks like Sly and Juice don't kick hard enough," I said. There had to be a half-dozen shirts lying between their beds.

"Hey, can I ask you a question?"

"Yeah, go ahead, man," I said. I opened my suitcase and started taking my things out.

"You said you were from New York, right?"

"Uh-huh." I hung up my suit.

"You from Harlem?"

"Yeah, that's right. Hey, I thought you said you put your clothes on the left side."

"Well, that's all I got," Colin said. "I got more, but they're just about the same thing. You don't need a whole lot of clothes living on a farm."

"What's it like living in . . . where did you say you come from?"

"Illinois. Cisne, Illinois."

"Yeah, what's it like living there?"

"I don't know, really," Colin said. "It's the only place I've ever lived. It's okay, I guess."

"Like Harlem," I said.

"How you figure like Harlem?" Colin asked me. "You ever been to Cisne?"

"No. But Harlem is the only place I've ever lived."

"Well, what we have is ten acres of played-out land," Colin said. "We tried to make a go of it, but it never did work out."

"What you mean played-out?" I asked.

"Can't grow anything on it," Colin said.

"What's it made of, rock?"

"Might as well be. You know anything about farming?"

"Nope."

"Well, you can't grow things in just any kind of dirt. You take sand, for example. You can't grow a thing in sand because it doesn't have anything to give to the plants. You keep growing crop after crop on a piece of land and after a while it just doesn't have anything left."

"Couldn't you put something on it?" I sat down on the bed. The dude was kind of interesting. "You know, like some vitamins or something?"

"That's like giving aspirin to a dead man," Colin said. "The funny thing was that we knew it wasn't going to work out, you know what I mean? But we kept working the land and working it until the bank came and told us that if we had anything worth taking, they would have taken it. We didn't have a damn thing worth taking. Almost killed Dad. That farm was the only thing he had in this world to give me."

"No lie?"

"Gospel truth."

I looked at Colin for a long moment and then went back putting my clothes in the closet. I had never seen a white cat this poor before.

"You think living in Harlem was about the same as living in Illinois?" Colin asked after a while.

"I don't know, man. You're white. There's no excuse for you being that poor."

"Oh, no?" Colin shook his head and laughed. "You know I told God that once."

"You did what?"

"Told God. One day this piece of tiller that we had broke down and Dad stayed up nearly all night trying to fix it. He got it to working, and the first thing in the morning he started out tilling, just a little way from the house. He must have been working five minutes when the thing died on him. Just like that. I still have the picture of it in my mind. Dad was laying over the wheel crying and pounding on the front of the tiller. I had never seen him so bad before. I was about seven at the time. That night I went and prayed to God and told him that we weren't supposed to be so bad off 'cause we were white. I had heard that black people were bad off and around Cisne you could see that most of them were, not all of them, though. Anyway, I swore I heard God answer me that night."

"Yeah, what did he say?"

"He said, 'Them's be the breaks, brother!' "

"You ain't got a bit of sense."

The next morning we were in the gym at eight thirty. They had already had a couple of practice sessions and I figured I'd be a little behind, but what bothered me more was hearing Colin and Juice talking about their chances of making the team. I had thought the scholarship meant that I would be on the team automatically. We suited up and shot baskets until the coaching staff arrived. They called me off the floor and assigned me a locker.

Montclare's locker room was deeply serious. They had a guy, a student, who was the team manager, and he assigned me a locker and gave me the combination to the lock. There was a carpet on the floor, a soda machine, an ice maker, rubdown tables, and just about everything else I could imagine that might be in a locker room, including a videotape machine. I got two practice uniforms, complete to socks, and a game uniform.

"You'll get a warm-up uniform if you make the

team," the manager said. "And you get a jacket after you score your first twenty-five points."

I was feeling good when I went out onto the floor for practice. The good feeling lasted about two minutes. They put us through stretching drills we were supposed to memorize, and then ball handling drills until we were just about too tired to stand. There were two coaches, Teufel and Leeds. Teufel had seen me play and had offered me the scholarship. But on the floor it seemed as if Leeds, the assistant coach, was the main man. After the drills he had us playing three men against four at three different baskets.

"There's two teams," he said, "a home team and a traveling team. The traveling team will be the nucleus of Montclare's basketball program and will consist of fifteen players. When we go on the road, these are the men who will go. The home team will be the traveling team and five more players. Under conference rules only fifteen players can suit up at any one time, but there will be five more players officially on the team. In case a player on the traveling team is hurt or sick, one of the five other players will suit up to take his place. All in all, there are twenty positions available, and if you look around you, you'll see that there are twenty-one players trying for these positions."

Leeds looked around with a big smile on his face like he was enjoying the whole thing.

There were three guys that Colin had told me about and I checked them out. One was a brother named Bobby Wortham that played center. I had heard about him because my cousin had played against him when the New York playground all-stars had played against the Philadelphia playground all-stars. I had seen him on television once when Montclare had played against DePaul's. He was smooth and handled the ball better than most big men.

The main guard, at least the one who made the most noise, was a stocky guy from Indiana named Hauser. Hauser had dirty-blond hair and gray eyes that never blinked. He wasn't much on going to the hoop but he could pass off either hand and hit from the outside. His best shot was on defense, though. He was quick and had real strong hands.

But the Montclare star was this long, lean dude who had made All-American the year before. Larson was thin in his body but he had big legs and he could really get up in the air. He could do anything that had to be done. Take you inside, take you to the corner, anything. He looked a little like the guy who played Superman in the movies, too, except that he had light brown eyes.

After the games Leeds asked us about injuries we'd had in the past, and if anybody needed their ankles taped for games. Then he went on about how they had computerized their offensive game and how each player was to accomplish certain goals. It didn't sound much like the kind of ball I had been playing most of my life.

Most of the team was white. There were four black guys, me, Bobby Wortham, a guy called Neil, and Juice. Juice was okay. He was a muscle guy with a big barrel chest. He wasn't too good-looking either, which made all those muscles seem for real. He wasn't really ugly, it was just that one side of his face always seemed to have a regular expression and the other half looked like it was mad or something.

Wortham came over and said hello to me and Juice and asked where we were from, but Neil acted as if he didn't even see us. His game was okay, he had a nice shot, but he acted a little as if he didn't want to get sweaty or something.

The rookies and the redshirts had to wait until the regulars had finished their showers before we could get into the shower room. I didn't mind that, but somehow I just didn't feel like I was part of what was going on. I was glad to get dressed and head back to Orly Hall. Sly caught up with me halfway there. He was six feet and had this hippy-dippy be-bop walk. He had dark hair, which he had cut short.

"What you think so far?" he asked.

I shrugged.

"Yeah," he said. "Same thing I was gonna say."

We exchanged fives.

2

They give me this little piece of job. I was supposed to work in a hospital which was about a mile away from the campus. It was called University Hospital. A lot of the kids who were studying to be doctors and whatnot, they worked in the hospital. What I was supposed to do was to work in the physical therapy department. Leeds said there wasn't much to the job, but I had to do it if I wanted to get some money for extra expenses, 'cause the scholarship only covered books and tuition and stuff and just enough money to get by on.

I got the campus bus and went over to the hospital. I found the physical therapy department after asking about six people directions. They looked at me as if

they had never seen a black guy before. Finally they
sent me down to the end of the building that looked a
little newer than the rest.

"Excuse me, I'm supposed to see Dr. Corbett."

The woman sitting behind the desk was kind of nice-
looking. I thought I had seen her around the campus
before but I wasn't too sure.

"You're Lonnie Jackson?" she asked. "The basketball player?"

"Yeah."

"I'm Ann Taylor." She stuck out her hand and I
shook it. "It's really Annie Taylor, but I hate Annie,
okay?"

"Hey, mama, it's your name."

"I hate mama, too."

"Yes, ma'am."

"Okay. Dr. Corbett isn't here right now, he's usually
here in the mornings. It's my understanding that
you're only going to be here six hours a week, right?"

"Right. Two days, three hours each day."

"Okay. Eddie Brignole comes twice a week, two and
a half hours each time. I think you can work with him."

"*You* think?"

"Dr. Corbett isn't too enthusiastic about the athletes working with the kids, but we're too shorthanded
to complain, really."

"Yeah, right."

"Let me tell you about Eddie. He's got one real
problem, as far as we know. Sometimes with a kid you
really can't tell what problems they have until they're
more developed. Anyway, Eddie's nine and he's so

withdrawn that at first we thought he was autistic, you know what I mean?"

"What does he do, draw and stuff like that?"

"Draw?" She had pretty eyes, man, and when she said that they got kind of wide and nice.

"No, he doesn't draw. He just sits around and does nothing most of the time. He won't play with the other kids or anything. Most of the time he just goes into the gym and sits by himself. What we do is just sit with him and talk to him. The staff psychiatrist seems to think that he looks forward to coming here even if he doesn't do anything and that it might help in the long run. Once in a while the athletes do get a rise from him, but not usually. So there you are."

"You said he'll be here soon?"

"Oh, one more little problem that you'll just love," Ann said. "Can I call you Lonnie?"

"Yeah."

"Eddie comes here with his mother. She sits in the gymnasium for the whole time. Whatever you do will be wrong as far as she is concerned. If she had the money she would take him to the—how does she put it now—'the best clinics in the world.' But she doesn't, so she's stuck with us, and we're stuck with her. She's not shy about telling you either."

"Okay," I said. "I guess I can handle it."

"I hope so. She's worn out two football players already."

I just sat around for a while and read and looked at a magazine until this kid Eddie was supposed to show up. After a while a woman about medium height with dark hair pulled away from her face with a comb and bobby pins at the back of her head came in. She wore a suede jacket with fur trim that fit her kind of nice. She probably could have looked a little better if she took care of herself. Ann motioned for me to come over. Well, this chick was sitting at the side of Ann's desk drumming her fingers like she was pissed off already.

"Mrs. Brignole, this is Lonnie Jackson." Ann's voice carried a smile with it. "He's going to be working with Eddie for a while."

"Hello." I stuck out my hand. She looked at it, and when she looked back at Ann she didn't make a move to shake my hand.

"Does he have experience working with young children?" she asked.

"Not at all," Ann said, smiling. "But I'm sure he'll do a wonderful job, Mrs. Brignole."

"If he has no experience, I don't want him working with Eddie," Mrs. Brignole said. "I insist upon having someone with some experience at least."

"Fine," Ann said. "We might get some experienced people in when the new budget is approved next spring. If and when we do, you'll be the first person we contact."

"I think . . . I think you're being impudent," Mrs. Brignole said.

"If you want to speak to Dr. Corbett, it's fine with me," Ann said. "He'll be in sometime tomorrow morning."

Mrs. Brignole took a deep breath and put her fingertips to her brow. Ann looked at her and then looked down at the desk. I started to say something like how I would try real hard, but Ann stopped me by raising her hand. I wasn't that interested in working with a handicapped kid in the first place.

"What am I supposed to do?" Mrs. Brignole spat each word out carefully. "Give my son over to any student who seems to have nothing to do?"

"I'm sorry, Mrs. Brignole," Ann said. "The only thing I can do is offer you what services we have. I don't want to sound uncaring, because I'm not, but you're going to have to take what we have to offer or wait until our budget is increased. Look, why don't you go and get Eddie, at least for today, and let him meet Lonnie."

Mrs. Brignole took a deep breath, stood, and walked out of the office.

"She don't seem too happy to see me," I said.

"She is not a happy woman," Ann answered.

"Look, is that it, she's just going now?"

"No, she has Eddie out in the car. She has this station wagon that looks like a World War Two tank. You know, the child has been like this for a long, long time. It's got to be hard on her, too, Lonnie. Dr. Corbett thinks it would help if she went through a little therapy herself, but she won't do it."

"She's a little wacky?" Lonnie asked.

"Probably not your out-and-out wack," Ann said. "But the home environment isn't right. A few hours here isn't going to help very much. But at least Eddie hasn't gotten worse."

"What do you do when he comes here? I mean, does he have a program?"

"No, he sits on the floor and he stays there for the

whole time unless there's a chair set up—then he sits on that."

"He sits down wherever you put the chair?"

"Wherever you put it," Ann said.

"Hey, look, what am I supposed to be doing with the dude?"

"Well, let him sit down on the chair and you could talk to him and you can do jumping jacks, anything. He will just look at you. If he responds to anything, which I don't think he will, then you can try to play on that. The whole thing is to try to get some response and, you know, other than that, you're just babysitting."

"Yeah, okay. Look, I'm going to check on the gym."

I went into the gym. It was a little dinky gym. I saw where the chairs were stacked against the one wall and I got one. I set it up and put it at the side of the foul lane under one basket. I saw a basketball and I went and got that.

Just then a door opened and Mrs. Brignole came in with Eddie. He was a little kid. Not even five feet tall. He looked a lot like his mother, except for his hair. Her hair was dark brown and his was like a red, a deep, dark red. I stood beneath the basket, just sort of bouncing the ball off the backboard. I watched as Eddie came slowly toward the chair and sat in it. Mrs. Brignole leaned against the wall.

"Do you want to sit there or do you want to get up and play some ball?" I asked.

Nothing.

The cat's face wasn't like blank, which is what I thought that Ann meant. Instead he just had his head down, like, you know, beaten, pushed down. I threw the basketball through the hoop and I looked at Eddie. The boy's head was still down.

"Okay," I said. "Now you sitting in that chair because somebody told you that you got to sit in that chair, right?"

Nothing.

"Now you got to look at what I'm doing for the same reason you got to sit in that chair, because if you don't look at me, then I don't know if you know what I'm doing, see. And you and me are going to get along. You can't make believe I ain't here. That's the only thing I don't like. Now you look at me, man."

Nothing.

Eddie kept his head down.

"Hey, I'm not going to keep telling you. When I tell you to look at me, I'm serious, man. I'm really serious."

Nothing.

I put the ball under my arm and walked over to the dude and lifted his chin up. I moved my arm and he let his head fall down to his chest again. I lifted it up again, the expression was the same. Now, I mean, he looked like he was sad, so I lifted his head a little harder.

"Hey, man, I ain't playing with your butt, stop ignoring me, man."

Out of the corner of my eye I could see his mama changing her position. I stood back and watched as my man's head dropped again and then I passed him the ball. It bounced lightly off his chest. I grabbed the ball and went up for a layup.

"Two nothing, my favor," I said. "Now it's your turn." I bounced the ball off of him again. "You missed an inbound pass, dude," I said, grabbing the ball. "I got it, I'll dribble around you, fake you out, and shoot. Yes! I got the ball in, that's four points for me and nothing for you. I'm going to wipe you up, turkey, you ain't no ballplayer."

I bounced the ball off Eddie's leg this time, grabbed it off the ground and started dribbling around him, faking left and faking right, then I leaned against Eddie's chair and turned around and put up a soft hook that touched nothing but net and fell through.

"All right. The kid is on his game," I said. "The television cameras are on me as I slaughter you, Eddieee. The score, nothing for you and six for meee."

I saw his mother take a step forward and stop. I see she is one of those protective mamas. I didn't care. I backed off a little bit and threw the ball to him, lightly.

"Here comes a pass to you." Bang. He didn't move and the ball rolled over to the side. I grabbed it.

"I got the rebound, now I'm going to dribble around you again and I'm going to fake you out. Here I come." I dribbled past him and laid the ball up again. "There, man. That's *ten* for me and nothing for you."

"Eight," came the voice from Eddie Brignole. "You only have eight."

"Okay, turkey," I said. "Eight. I thought I could beat you a little easier than that. I see you watching everything I do, huh. Okay, this time I'm not going to announce the game, man. I'm just going to go on and shoot the ball, man. 'Cause you got your head down and you won't be seeing what I be doing, man. Okay, here comes the ball to you." I threw him the ball. It bounced off of him again. I grabbed it and moved toward the basket, but this time I was watching him and he turned just as I threw the ball against the backboard. It fell through.

"Now I got ten, now I got ten!" Then I came back, threw him the ball again. I saw his hand move, he wanted to grab it. I just knew he wanted to grab that ball.

I said, "Okay, okay, Eddie, now the game is twenty. I got ten in the first half. But right now I'm going to show you a few shots, right? I'm going to amaze you. Watch this."

I moved back to the top of the key. I looked at him to see if he was looking at me. He wasn't looking right at me but he had lifted his head and I knew he could see me out of the corner of his eye. I put the ball on the floor one time and I threw up a soft jump shot. It arched easily through the air and bounced off the back rim. I looked over at Eddie and he smiled.

"Hey, man, don't be smiling at me. I mean, I could still beat you, even if I did miss that one shot."

It went on like that for about a half hour more. The dude was actually glad to see me miss and I didn't care. It was like a little game we were playing. He was sitting there watching me, hoping I would miss and I was watching him, seeing how he would react. Then I told him we would have a rest period and we would start the second half of our game, but this time I told him I wanted him to get up off that chair and try a shot. All you got to do is try one shot, just one shot and that's all, okay, one shot?

"Can you make one shot? Oh, I see you can't even make one shot, that's your problem, man."

He didn't say anything. I sort of picked him up in one arm, half lifted him, and walked him over to the basket. I knew he could walk okay. I put the basketball in his hands and lifted it, and I told him very softly in his ear, "Don't drop this ball when I give it to you, man. Don't drop this ball, 'cause I ain't like those other people, man, you know. I'm black and mean, jim. So don't drop this basketball."

I put it in his hand and he held it for a long moment.

"Go on shoot it, go on shoot it."

He threw the ball up, it hit the bottom of the rim and fell down. I grabbed it and I kept on playing like I had before when he was sitting down. I would grab it and dribble around him. He just stood there. I kept throwing him the ball but he would just let it bounce off his body.

I said, "Okay, man."

I figured I would see what this dude was really made of. I had an idea what he was made of when I saw the smile when I missed the shot and when he corrected me on the score. The dude didn't like losing. He didn't like losing, I knew.

I said, "Okay, Eddie, tell you what I'm going to do, man. Since I'm on the basketball team and you're not even on a basketball team, I guess you need a little break, so I'm going to give you a break. Here, I'm going to give you the basketball and walk all the way across the gym now. If you make a basket before I get back over to you, I'm going to give you ten points.

Now hold this basketball, Eddie, HOLD THE BAS-
KETBALL. I told you I'm black and mean, jim."

He took the basketball. I didn't have to lift his arms.
I walked all the way across the floor, turned, and said,
"Okay, Eddie, here I come now." I began walking
slowly toward him. He didn't move. I kept on coming,
very slowly. "Here I come, Eddie, here I come. You
better get it up now. You better get it up. If you want
them ten points you better get it up, here I come."

"Don't intimidate him."

This is from his mother. She started from the other
direction.

"She must be on your side, Eddie. Here she comes
to help you."

She moved faster and I moved faster. Eddie shifted
his feet. "Don't intimidate him, don't intimidate my
son. You don't know a thing about . . ."

I jumped in front of her as she neared her son. She
tried to get around me, but I kept blocking her out,
blocking her out.

"She must be on your side."

"What are you doing? Are you crazy . . . are you
cra— What are you doing?"

"I know you want to pass the ball to her, Eddie, but I
won't let you do it, man. I'm not going to let you do it,
man."

"You get out of my way."

Eddie turned and threw the ball up against the backboard. The ball rolled around the rim and I said a
quick, quick prayer. "Lord, PLEASE, let it roll in."

The Lord did a cool thing, as the ball fell through
the hoop.

Eddie looked up at the basket and then he glanced over at me.

"Good shot," I said. "You got a nice touch."

I went and got the ball. Eddie's mother stood still for a long moment in the middle of the floor, and then she went back to where she had been standing near the wall. I didn't try to force Eddie to shoot anymore, and he didn't. Once, when the ball landed near him, he picked it up, held it for a second or two, and then threw it to me.

I felt relaxed with Eddie. I felt like just hanging around the gym with him and shooting baskets. I didn't know exactly how Eddie felt, but I knew that at that moment, standing in a gym in Indiana, he wasn't feeling great about himself. I knew the feeling.

3

"The subject, ladies and gentlemen"—I watched Dr. Weiser as he wrote his name on the blackboard—"is American history, and I am teaching it. That's Dr. Weiser, W-E-I-S-E-R. Many of you believe that you know a great deal about American history, but let me assure you that you don't. When you leave my class, however, you will understand the subject."

The desks were arranged so that we were all looking down at Dr. Weiser. He leaned back in his chair and put his feet on the desk. I looked around to see if there were any other blacks in the room. I spotted three. One guy from the football team, a big heavy guy from

Alabama, looked like a mountain. There was a guy with horn-rimmed glasses and a cute brown-skinned girl who sat near the front of the room.

"American history is a sadly neglected subject," Dr. Weiser went on. "Many people feel that because our history does not extend as far back as European history, it somehow doesn't have the same merit. I feel just the opposite. I feel that because it is relatively short we can get a better grasp on it than we can, say, on the history of older countries. Plus, the importance of American history is often overlooked. We have in the two hundred or so years of our existence influenced the world more than any other culture in the known history of man. As far as this point in time is concerned, there is no other history as relatively important as our own, an opinion with which, I am sure, you will all soon come to agree."

Dr. Weiser stood up and began walking around the room. Some feet started shuffling under the chairs.

"I see that Mr. Jenkins and Mr. Smith are with us again."

Dr. Weiser walked up to the football player and shook his hand. I could tell that the football player didn't want to shake Dr. Weiser's hand. Then he walked up to a white guy and shook his hand.

"Mr. Jenkins and Mr. Smith were with us last year for American history, but somehow didn't feel that they had to learn it then." Dr. Weiser smiled.

I could definitely tell this was a guy I was not going to like.

"They felt," Dr. Weiser went on, "that because they were athletes it wouldn't be required of them to learn how their country was formed. It was an unfortunate situation; therefore, it has become necessary for them to repeat this course, and if they decide somewhere along the line this year that they do not have to learn the subject, I am sure that they will see fit to repeat the course again. I understand that we have two other athletes in the class. I would strongly advise them to consider the case of Mr. Jenkins and Mr. Smith and learn what I expect from *all* of my students regardless of their musculature, regardless of their ability to run, or to jump, or to do whatever it is they do in the course of the triviality in which they choose to engage."

I looked at the white guy and tried to imagine what he played. He wasn't big enough for football. And I hadn't seen him on the basketball squad. Maybe he played baseball.

Weiser went on about what books to buy and then gave us a long reading assignment. Then he went into a lecture about the reasons why Europeans had chosen to come to America instead of Africa or the East Indies.

"Believe it or not," Dr. Weiser said, "some of the African countries were more civilized than the United States in many respects; however, at that juncture of history it was the European culture that was in the ascendancy, and any culture that was not touched by it suffered a period of stagnation. Stagnation, I might add, that still afflicts India and much of Africa."

I saw some of the other students taking notes. I wrote down a few things myself, but the cat was talking so fast I didn't know what was going on. The girl in front of me was writing a mile a minute. I couldn't figure out what she was putting down in her notebook. Also, I was wondering how much of the stuff that he was talking about I was supposed to know. When he finally ended the class with a little dig at the athletes, hey, I felt glad.

I was supposed to go to basketball practice, then to a psychology class. When I first got to Montclare and registered for classes, I told myself that I was going to really do it. I was going to buckle down and do this heavy education number and not jive around like I did in high school. But after taking Dr. Weiser's class, and seeing how this dude was so cold, I had my doubts. I tried to get it out of my head as I walked out of the class.

"Hey, what's your name?"

I turned and saw the brown-skinned girl who had been sitting in front of the history class. I nodded to her. My mind was still on how I was going to make it here at Montclare.

"You do have a name?" she asked.

"Yeah, yeah, hey, I'm sorry. I got a name, it's Lonnie."

"Lonnie Jackson, right?"

"Yeah, how did you know?"

"My name is Sherry, Sherry Jewett," she said, "and I work in the administration office. I checked out all the athletic scholarships to see if there were any bloods. I figured you were a blood 'cause you were on the basketball team. You're from New York, right?"

"Yeah, right. You have a thing for athletes or something?"

"You remember Dr. Weiser making that crack about there being two other athletes in the class?"

"Yeah, I heard it."

"I'm the other one."

"You? You're an athlete?"

"That's right. I'm an athlete."

"What do you do? I mean, you know, you play volleyball or something?"

"I run track."

"Oh, you any good?"

"Yeah, I'm some good," she said. "I'm some good."

"I thought you would be, as fine as you are and everything."

"Oh, come on, all right?"

"Okay. Your show, mama. Where you from?"

"Milwaukee."

"Milwaukee? I didn't know they had black people in Milwaukee. I mean, they don't have that many, right?"

"There must be a wall around New York or something," Sherry said. "You have got the most *ignorant* people in New York City."

"Hey, we'll do," I said.

"Anyway, I'm trying to get a study group up with some of the black athletes. So far I have spoken to ten. There are twenty-five in all. There are only three freshmen, including you and Juice. You want to join?"

"Yeah, I guess so," I said. "How many people are in it so far?"

"Two." Sherry smiled. "The rest don't have the time. Are you in Orly Hall?"

"Yeah."

"Okay, I'll check you out later. See how many more people I can get together."

"Hey, how come you're doing this?" I called after her as she started away.

" 'Cause it sounds like a good idea," Sherry said. "So I thought I'd do it."

"All right, okay." I watched as she cut across the grass toward some white girls headed for the science building. She caught up with them, and in a moment they were all talking. She was really fine. She had to be at least five feet seven, or five feet eight. That kind of soft brown complexion that always turned my head a little bit. But the best thing about her was her smile. She had a wide mouth and full sensuous lips, the nicest dimples I had ever seen in my entire life. I couldn't imagine her doing no heavy athletic number.

I got to the gym and practice was stiff, lifeless, man. I had these figures in mind that Leeds told me I had to get before the practice began. "We are going to have a scrimmage game," he had said. "You have to get seven rebounds and five assists in the scrimmage."

"Yeah, okay, right, bet."

They had some plays they wanted to work on. One of them had Sly going to the corner and passing it out to Larson, cutting across the high post. They didn't tell the whole play, they just told Sly to go out and pass the ball to Larson. But Sly's man heard the whole thing and he kept backing off Sly and waiting for him to make the pass so he could switch to Larson. But Sly faked the pass and threw a jumper, which went cleanly through the net. They ran the play a second time and the same thing happened. Coach Teufel blew his whistle and asked Sly if he had a problem.

"No, man," Sly said. "But I'm open for the shot and the cat is laying off of me so I had to put it up."

"You have to put it up again," Coach Teufel said, "and you won't be putting it up for *this team* anymore, do you understand that?"

"I do indeed understand it, Mr. Boss," Sly said.

The rest of the practice was even more nothing, with the team running plays for Larson and only Hauser being allowed to drive, unless it was a set play. I didn't even get to work up a sweat during that part of the practice. Then they went into a scrimmage game and, hey, that was okay. They put all the regulars against the rookies and they just about tore us up. But I still got some of my stuff off. I tried to remember those figures that Leeds gave me. But after a while I just forgot them and went on and played my game. We lost the scrimmage, but I felt okay because I thought I had done all right.

Sly was good. He had a lot of moves and went to the hoop as strongly as anybody I had ever seen. Juice was strong inside, but he wasn't that quick. I could see him backing off plays and going for the rebound when he should have been trying to stuff his man. He had a nice outside shot but he wasn't quick enough for anybody to let him play outside.

Colin surprised me. His game looked a little awkward, but he didn't miss anything either from outside or inside. When he walked on the court it looked like he was coming to take care of some heavy business, and he did it.

It wasn't a good kind of ball, I could tell. Playing ball had always been the most important thing in my life. What it had always been about, what it was still about, was beating another man. You had to be quicker, and stronger, and able to concentrate better than whoever it was you were playing against. I had seen coaches like Leeds before. Coaches that talked about running patterns on the floor and setting up screens and a lot of other things that made it a team sport. But a good offensive team would always be neutralized by a good defensive team if it wasn't for the idea that some guys could do more with the ball. Whoever held them would be beat often enough to throw the team defense off. People who couldn't do the things on the floor, people like Leeds, were still trying to make it into their kind of game.

After the scrimmage I took a shower and put my clothes back on. Larson came over to me.

"Hey, man, you got any money?"

"Couple of dollars," I said.

"Look," Larson said. "We got a little thing that we do every year. There's these guys out at the mill and we play them a few games. We play for twenty dollars a man. If you want to play, I'll put you up."

"Twenty dollars a man? Who are these dudes, man?"

"They're just a bunch of stiffs, jim. Every year they play us a few games. They lose their money and they're happy."

"Hold time, hold time, if they lose every year, why they playing?"

"They're like groupies, man. They play and then

they can sit back a little later on and watch us on television and say 'I played against these dudes.' You know, it helps them get their dreams off."

"It's that easy, huh?"

"Hey, we can take them, man, it's no big deal."

"Well, I got a psychology class," I said. "I don't think I can make it. When you say you playing?"

"About an hour from now."

"No, I can't make it, man."

"Who you got for psychology, Mrs. King?"

"Yeah."

"No sweat, man. Everybody passes her class. Come on. You can play."

"Who's all playing?"

"A couple of guys from the team and this guy who hangs around the team sometime, named Ray," Larson said. "Don't say anything around Leeds or the coach. We're playing this team on the q.t. They're kind of physical and the coaches are afraid we'll get an injury. But the way I figure, twenty bucks is twenty bucks."

I said, "Okay." I didn't really want to play that much, but another thing I didn't want to do was go to any more classes that day.

We played outdoors in a playground. There were a lot of factories around the playground but it really wasn't run-down or anything like that. The team we were supposed to play was already there, warming up. They were older guys. Most of them were dressed in dungarees and sweat shirts. They didn't look like much. Too short and too heavy to be playing against us. We warmed up for about five minutes. I didn't recognize any of the guys that were on our team. As soon as Larson gave me their names I forgot them. They were all younger guys, but they looked like ballplayers anyway.

Except for one older brother, I remembered his name. It was Ray. We started the game with him taking the ball out. The winner was the first team to reach twenty baskets. When one team reached ten baskets, we would change sides and that would be the half.

When they took the ball out I could tell right away that it was no contest. They were slow and none of them were that good. But Larson was right, they did beat the heck out of us physically. Every time you grabbed the ball you would get hit at least twice. You had to call your own foul because we didn't have a referee and the most you could get was to take the ball out of bounds. They kept up with us for a long while, just beating on us. But the brother named Ray, he kept them off our backs pretty good. He looked at them a lot and swung elbows with them under the boards.

I noticed Larson played it cool. We got out in front of them on a series of fast breaks and Larson told us to cool it. Keep the score down so they would play us again. I said, "Okay, sure." I could use the twenty dollars. The pocket money I got from the school was just about gone and I wasn't supposed to get paid for working at the hospital until the end of the month. They made a little comeback, but it wasn't enough. At the end of the game my arms were sore from the beating they gave us, but we had won. We all shook hands and they started to leave, thanking us for the game. I went over to where Larson sat against the fence taking off his sneakers.

"Hey, man, what happened to the bread?"

"You'll get it," he said. "Don't worry about it."

"Yeah, okay."

Larson said that he was going to go get his car, which he had parked about a block or so away. I was still thinking about the money, wondering if I had been conned, but I just played along with the program.

"Hey, you got a nice game, brother." Ray, little drops of sweat collecting on his brows and dripping down into his face, came over. "You got a real nice game."

"You're the man," I said. "I thought they were going to do it to us for a while."

"They just rough," Ray said. "You know, they try to intimidate you. Beat on you and whatnot. A lot of them played ball for different schools a few years ago, and that bald dude even played pro for a while."

"That bald dude with the set shot?"

"Yeah. He's in his forties now, but he played pro for a while. He spent some time on the bench in Cleveland, but he was still pro."

"Where did you play?"

The brother took his wallet from his pocket and pulled a square patch of plastic from it. He unfolded the plastic and I saw that there was a yellowed newspaper clipping in it. He did the whole thing so carefully, I could tell it was important to him. He wiped his hand on his sweat pants and handed me the clipping.

Ray York, All America candidate, scored thirty points as Montclare upset a highly favored Purdue team. The Boilermakers found themselves in early foul trouble but it was York's rebounding and scoring under the offensive boards that set up the last second shot possibility which eventually won the game as Powers scored at the buzzer in the 86–84 upset.

"Hey, I didn't know you played for Montclare," I said.

"I don't make a big thing of it," Ray said, taking the clipping and refolding it into the plastic. "I still work out with the team once in a while."

"When did you graduate?" I asked.

"I had a little trouble." Ray was leaning against the fence. "Got a girl pregnant and had to go out and work. I'm thinking about playing some ball in Europe. I heard they pay pretty nice."

"Yeah, I heard that, too," I said. "Some dudes from the Knicks went over there last year."

"I haven't really made up my mind," Ray said. "I might do some coaching. I figure whatever I get into I want to stick with, that's why I'm hanging here at the mill until I make a decision."

"I can dig it," I said. I watched Ray put the clipping back into his wallet and put his wallet away.

"Look, I gotta split." Ray looked at his watch. "The old lady probably wants me to do some shopping. You know how that domestic thing goes."

"Yeah, take care, man."

We exchanged fives and I watched him as he left. He

took one of the balls and went down the street with it under his arm. I remembered my friend Cal, who had played in the NBA. He had shown me a scrapbook full of clippings, laughing all the while about how skinny he had been during his playing days. Things had worked out a lot differently for Ray. I wondered if he had more than that one sad clipping. Then I put it out of my mind.

Larson pulled his car around and I got in next to him.

"That Ray is all right," I said. "You know he played for Montclare."

"He's all right for this kind of game," Larson said, pulling away from the curb. "You know, elbows, shoving, that kind of thing."

"You got to be kidding me," I said. "That cat's good. He can play any kind of ball."

"Maybe," Larson said, hunching forward slightly over the steering wheel. "Anyway, the Fat Man likes him."

"Who?"

"The Fat Man. Hey, you got to meet the Fat Man," Larson said without looking at me. "He really knows basketball. Every once in a while he gets us a game off campus. He got us our first games with these guys. He scouts the teams and everything. Most of the time we play for five or ten dollars a man and we can only play seven guys. But once we played for three hundred."

"For what?"

"Three hundred a man," Larson said. "There was this team from Michigan that came to Indiana to play in a tournament. They wiped out the tournament and the Fat Man arranged for them to play us. He put up the money and bet on us."

"I know that Teufel doesn't know anything about that kind of action," I said. "He'd probably put you off the team if he did."

"He knows," Larson said. "All that week he had us practicing traps. I couldn't figure out why. Ray worked out with us, too. When we got to the game we found out they had this squad that averaged like six five."

"*Averaged* six five?"

"Yep. But they didn't have a ball handler."

"And so you trapped them all night."

"Now you got it," Larson said. "Hey, look, you want to meet the Fat Man? We're going by his place."

"I don't know, maybe some other time."

"Well, listen," Larson said, "I have to stop there anyway."

"Yeah, okay."

Carmine's Pizza Heaven was in the center of town. There were three pizza makers who stood in front of a large plate glass window and kneaded and tossed the dough.

Larson motioned for me to follow him as he entered the shop. We went right past the booths filled with pink-legged high school girls and muscular farm boys with bad teeth that glowered at me as I went by them and through the swinging doors into the back.

"Hey, Fat Man, we beat the mill boys again today." Larson was talking to this real fat dude sitting on a stool in the corner of the kitchen.

"How much you play them for?" Fat Man asked.

"Twenty," Larson said. "If I could play those guys every day I'd quit school tomorrow."

"Then you would be a fool," Fat Man said. "Education is what you got one chance to get. After a while you get dumber and dumber, and if you ain't got an education before then you too dumb to get one."

"Yeah, that figures," Larson said. "Hey, I want you to meet Lonnie. He's from New York. He's not a bad ballplayer for a freshman."

I reached out my hand to shake the Fat Man's. He looked me up and down and then slowly extended his hand.

"Carmine," he said. His fingers were almost as big around as my wrist. "But you can call me Fat Man. Mostly because everyone else does. Anytime you want a good pizza, you come on by here. We make the best pizza outside of New York and we don't charge too much. People around here are getting good pizzas and don't even know it."

"Yeah," I said.

"When are you getting us a big game?" Larson asked.

"You want to play next week?" Fat Man asked. "Next Friday? I can get you a game with a team from the post office over in Muncie, fifty dollars a man."

"With the post office?" I looked at the Fat Man.

"Yeah," Fat Man answered without looking back at me. "They think they're good. A good high school team could beat them. A guy that runs a used car lot over there is backing them. The only thing, you can't play, Larson."

"How come?" Larson looked hurt.

"I don't want you to play over there 'cause of the publicity," Fat Man said. "They'll write you up because the drunk that has the used-car lot is beating the drums to get publicity for his hustle. If you don't play, the most he gets is some talk around the neighborhood; you play, and it gets wrote up in the local rag and right away it looks like you're taking advantage, which you are. You can coach if you want to. Get that guy, the colored guy, what's his name . . . Ray, to play and maybe that skinny guy from the mill, let him win for a change."

"I'll think about it," Larson said. "I'll let you know."

Me and Larson went out front and ordered a slice of pizza and some sodas.

"Hey, how come he sets the games up and stuff?" I asked Larson.

"Look, you might as well get used to it," Larson said. "As long as you're playing ball for a school like Montclare they're going to be a lot of people trying to hang on to your coattails. Now chicks, they hang around you and they try to get you into the sack just so they can say 'Hey, you know, I made it with a ballplayer.' Guys, they'll either try to buy you dinner or drinks or, like the Fat Man, he sets up games for us. That's how he gets off."

"Yeah?" I looked at him. "And speaking of setting up games, man, I thought we were supposed to be playing for some bread today."

"Oh, yeah." Larson began to fish around in his pocket. "I don't usually pay off until the next day," Larson said. "I don't want to get in trouble for a gambling rap. You pay off right away, you get guys clamoring around for their bread, and bingo, somebody starts talking about getting in on the action and you got something you can't handle. I don't need it."

"I thought you said Teufel knows about it."

"He knows, man, and he don't know, okay? Let's put it like that. As long as he don't know the details, then everything's cool."

I got the twenty bucks from Larson and he gave me a ride back to the campus. I didn't much like the talk with the Fat Man about betting on games. But it really wasn't the school team that was playing. It was just a pickup game and didn't mean anything. I told myself that twice before we got back to Orly Hall.

4

Colin had this guitar that he would play when he studied. Sometimes he would prop his books up on the bed and sit on the floor and just look at them while he strummed. I didn't exactly hate his guitar playing, but I didn't exactly love it, either. Sly couldn't stand country and western, which is what Colin played mostly.

"Hey, man." Sly was sitting with a towel wrapped like a turban around his head with a bowl of peanuts in front of him. "You ever get down with some real music, Colin?"

Colin played a few bluesy bars and then slipped back into his country and western.

"Can you play any George Benson?" Sly asked.

"What are you doing with those peanuts?" I asked Sly. He was fooling around with them one by one.

"I'm brushing the salt off of them," Sly said. "All salt is cursed. It'll kill you just like that!"

"You out your mind," I said.

"Hey, Colin," Sly went on, "really, can you play any George Benson?"

Colin played a few bars from something and Sly got all excited. He told me to lay down some rhythm and I slapped my hand on a book and he started making a hornlike noise.

"Yo, we can be good!" Sly said. "You can play guitar, Lonnie on skins, me on horn, and we'll put my man Juice on bass."

"You read music?" Colin asked.

"I don't read it," Sly said, closing his eyes, "I *feel* it floating through the universe."

"Reading helps," Colin said.

"What do you say, Lonnie?" Sly threw his sneaker toward me. "You want to start a group? We can be the Montclare Jazz Quartet."

"Does Juice play the bass?" I asked.

"I don't know," Sly said, "but the dude looks like a bass player, don't he?"

"How about instruments?" Colin was interested, I could tell. "You have a horn?"

"You have a guitar, that's a start," Sly said. "And I was checking out the music store in town. They got this jellybean counting contest. Whoever comes closest gets a free instrument."

"Naturally we're going to win it." I looked at Sly hanging over the side of his bed.

"Naturally," he said. "And with me as creative director, my man Colin as musical director, and Lonnie as business manager, we'll be famous in about six months."

"How about Juice?" I asked.

"He ain't here, so we'll make him equipment manager," Sly said.

The phone rang and it was Sherry asking if I wanted to walk her down to the track. I said okay and told her I'd meet her in front of the building.

"Where you going, man?" Sly asked. "We're having the first creative conference of the Montclare Jazz Quartet now."

"I'm walking Sherry down to the track," I said, grabbing my jacket from the back of a chair.

"Is she more important than the future of American music?" Colin asked.

"I don't know," I said. "She got this little study group going. Half the people in it don't show up most of the time. Anyway, she's got this idea that if somebody reads you something from a book, it's better than if you read it yourself. So she's reading from the history book and I'm sitting there thinking that this girl might be more important than a lot of things."

"So what you're telling me," Colin said in this real serious voice, "is that you're basically interested in the young lady's intellectual ability."

I grinned.

Sherry had the baddest warm-up suit I had ever seen. The material was white and fuzzy and made her look fat, which she wasn't. She started over toward the track and she showed me how to use the stopwatch she had.

"I want to run one-minute quarters," she said. "What I have to do is to get the pace right."

We got to the track and she started doing stretching exercises. First she sat down and touched her head to her knees a few times, then she stood up and touched the ground with her palms.

"You really have to warm up good in track," she said, slipping out of her warm-up suit. "It's so easy to tear a muscle. You wouldn't mind helping me, would you?"

"No," I said.

"Sit in front of me," she said, sitting on the ground with her legs apart, "like this."

I sat on the ground in front of her with my legs apart and she put her feet against mine.

"Now, I'm just going to push against you, okay?" She put her hands on the ground in back of her and lifted herself on the ground just a little as she pushed forward, stretching her legs farther and farther apart. "I'm not sure how flexible you are, so if I hurt you, let me know."

"Hey, this is just fine with me," I said as she pushed herself even closer.

"I usually do this with one of the girls on the track team," Sherry said, half closing her eyes, "but they don't do it as well as you do. Have you had a lot of practice stretching people out?"

"I ain't had no whole lot of practice, but this is definitely something I could get used to," I said.

"Bet you could, too," she said, smiling.

She got up before I could say anything else and started around the track. She went easily, clapping her hands in front of her every few steps. When she got back, she said she was ready for me to time her.

As soon as she got on the track she seemed to change. All the cute little things she was doing with the stretching and peeling off the warm-up suit had stopped. She was all business.

I checked the watch once more to make sure that I knew how to start it, then I got her on the mark.

"Go!"

She really took off. Her legs weren't moving that fast, but her stride was long and graceful and I could see she had some power. I looked at the clock. She did the first half of the quarter in thirteen and a half seconds, and the second half in twenty-eight and a half seconds. I looked up and watched as she leaned into the far turn. Just past the turn she seemed to slow down a bit. She got the curve a little slow and then picked it up as she hit the top of the straightway, ending the quarter a second over one minute. She rested for a minute and then went again. She ran six quarters over the next half hour, finishing each within two seconds of the one minute she was shooting for.

"Not bad, girl," I said, when she finished what she had said was to be her last quarter.

"I'm doing the first part of it too quickly," she said. "I'm going to have to work on it."

She put on her top and threw me the pants to carry.

"You look pretty good to me," I said.

"The coach wants me to switch to the four forty," she said. "I don't want to."

"How come?"

"They want me and this Puerto Rican girl, Yolande, to run the sprints because they figure we'll need less training than the white girls on the team for sprints. Everybody needs training for the mile, so they want to make us run sprints and them run the middle distances. But if you're good, you have a better chance of making the Olympic team in the middle or long distances than you do in the sprints," she said. "It's better for the team, but it's not better for me. It's not even good for me."

"And you're good," I said.

"I told you I was, didn't I?" she said. She smiled, took her warm-up pants from me, put them on, and stretched out on the grass.

"Yeah, yeah, you told me," I said. "All I can see is how sweet you are."

"Lonnie, do me a favor, please. Don't start it."

"Don't start what?"

"Don't start hitting on me, okay? I mean just cool out."

"What's all this mess? You running around talking about you going to get the brothers and the sisters together for a study group and all of this stuff and now I can't even talk to you, right?"

"I just don't want to talk to you like that, Lonnie. Don't you have an old lady at home, anyway?"

"No, man, you know. I was kinda playing the field."

"I thought that all you New York guys had steady girlfriends," Sherry said.

"No, I think I made a big mistake when I was in the city. I was fooling around, fooling with this girl and that girl and then all of a sudden I found myself all alone and I didn't want to be all alone. When I realized that I wanted somebody to be with, more than just the 'hey, hey, how you doing' kind of thing, I was ready to leave the city and come out here to Montclare. You know, I kinda wish I had somebody to write back home to. I bet you got an old man?"

"No, I guess not."

"What do you mean you guess not?"

"Well, I had a boyfriend in high school and we broke off over the last summer. He wanted me to go to Michigan State with him. I didn't want to go to Michigan State and so he said that was the end of our relationship. It wasn't that heavy anyway."

"Why didn't you want to go to Michigan State?"

" 'Cause that's where he was going. That's all. I mean, I spent two and a half years doing what he wanted to do. If he wanted to go to the movies, I went to the movies. If he wanted to go to the ball game, I went to the ball game. I just did not want to go to Michigan State, that's all."

"It looks like we in the same boat, then," I said. "Neither one of us has anybody heavy, so you know, maybe we can get together."

"Well, we'll see."

She was still lying there on the grass and I reached over and put my fingertips against her lips. She flashed a quick smile and then rolled over and hopped to her feet.

"Do you want to take a walk?"

"No, why do I want to take a walk? What I really want to do is to kiss you."

"Lonnie, please, *please*. Can't it be something light?"

"Hey, man, what . . . I'm not good enough for you?"

"I didn't say that. . . . Look, I have a great idea. Why don't you go back to the dorm or someplace."

"Yeah, okay, hey . . . no big deal, mama. You know, if that's how you feel about it."

I got up and walked away. I went back to Orly, where Colin was still strumming his guitar. Sly was on the bed practicing cheating at cards.

"Hey, Lonnie, come on and play me some acey-deucey."

"Man, get out of here," I said to Sly.

"Come on, Lonnie."

Sly took some one-dollar bills out of his pocket and threw them on the bed.

"You could take all my money, man. Come on, Lonnie."

"I'll play you one game," I said, "for one dollar."

"Hey, now you talking, bro."

I sat down on the edge of the bed and watched Sly shuffle and deal the cards. He turned up an ace and a three for me.

"You care to double your bet, man? That looks good."

Against my own better judgment I threw in another dollar. Sly turned over a deuce. Snatched up my two dollars and howled with laughter.

I picked up the cards and threw them at him and then went and laid back on my bed. It bothered me what had happened with Sherry, because I knew she didn't want me to hit on her and I just about knew that she was going to say no when I told her I wanted to kiss her. I had been thinking about Sherry a lot. Thinking about what I would say to her and how I would act around her. Colin was right, she was smart, I knew that. I could see that, but there was more, too. I wasn't used to dealing with girls outside of a man-and-woman thing. I didn't know how to just hang out and rap, or do casual things. It made me feel bad, in a way, and in another way it got me mad. I knew I wasn't supposed to be mad at her, she didn't do anything to me, but when I was with her I ended up feeling bad about myself.

I fell across my bed and closed my eyes. I was mad at Sherry because I didn't know what to do with her, and mad at Sly for ripping off my two dollars, and getting pretty tired of hearing Colin's guitar.

The phone rang and Sly got it, just as Juice came in the door.

"If that's the president, tell him I'm too busy to talk to his butt," Juice said.

Sly looked at me and asked me was I in.

"Who is it?" I asked.

"Some girl named Sherry."

"Yeah, I'm in," I said.

"Hello?"

"Hi, Lonnie."

"Hi, Sherry. Nice of you to talk to the little people."

"Lonnie, please . . . I am trying . . . to get along with you."

"Hey, don't put yourself out, girl. What did you want?"

"They're going to have *The Island* at the Quad this

Friday. It's an old Japanese movie I've been dying to see," she said. "If you don't think I'm absolutely terrible, maybe you'll take me."

"Yeah, why not," I said. I had already taken Sherry to one of the old movies she had been "dying" to see and had hated the sucker.

"Fine, Mr. Jackson," she said. "I'll see you Friday."

"Yeah, sure."

I hung up the phone and lay back down on the bed. When Sly had said that it was Sherry, I felt good about it, but as soon as I got on the phone I just about blew it. I definitely did not know how to talk to the girl.

5

I got to practice and I dug that a few dudes weren't there that had been there the day before. Before we ran through our drills Teufel got us all together and started rapping about how we were representing the school and how we had to keep that in mind and whatnot. Then we went into layup drills.

"Yo, Lonnie." Sly was behind me in the drill. "You dig some cats ain't here?"

"Yeah."

"Leeds called them over this morning and told them they didn't make the squad. Everybody here made it."

"We did?" I looked at him and saw that he was serious. "How come he didn't just out and say it?"

"Probably would have broke his heart," Sly said. He cut in front of me, got the ball, and let it roll off his fingertips into the hoop. The dude was definitely smooth.

Our first game was at home against St. Louis, and they weren't anything special. Before the game Teufel and Leeds were saying that we wanted to run as many set plays as possible and keep the game under control.

The coach started Hauser and McKinney as the guards, Neil and Larson up front and Wortham at center. No way St. Louis was going to keep up with them. They ran the score to twenty-four to ten before you could blink twice.

"Look, man, when we get in we're going to have to show something." Juice was sitting next to me on the bench.

"Teufel was saying he wanted to run the plays we practiced," I said.

"Uh-huh, that's what he said," Juice said. "But Larson told me that he has to decide who's on the traveling team before our first conference game. He said if the freshmen don't show well, put the redshirts on the traveling team."

I was pretty sure that I was going to make the traveling team. The redshirts were mostly big guys who could rebound a little but didn't have much of an all-around game. One guy was on the football team and I thought he was on the squad just to say he got a letter in basketball and football. I wasn't too sure how Juice was going to make out.

By the end of the first half the score was forty-two to twenty-six, but the game wasn't even that close. St.

Louis was a small school that didn't have the kind of basketball program that Montclare did. In the locker room Teufel was saying that anyone that didn't get in during the first half would probably get a chance to play in the second half. He talked some more about running the plays we had practiced, but I didn't notice them running that many set plays in the first half.

In the second half I started with Hauser in the back court, and Juice and Larson played up front. This big white boy from Scranton, Pennsylvania, played center. He had just become eligible and was new to the squad. His name was Joseph Gogosky but everybody called him Go-Go.

We hustled the entire second half. Teufel put Sly, Skipper and some of the other guys in, but I stayed in for the whole half. Most of the hustle, though, came from Larson. During practice he seemed to loaf a little. Even when we had played the mill guys he wasn't doing that much. But when we played St. Louis, he hustled every minute he was in. The rest of us went along with him. Cats were diving for loose balls, fighting for rebounds, the whole thing. At the end of the game I was really tired, but we had won ninety-six to sixty-three. Some of the guys from St. Louis were ticked off because we had pressed so hard even after we had the game in the bag. Their coach even walked off the floor without shaking Teufel's hand after the game.

We felt good about the game. The only surprise, as far as I was concerned, was how well Go-Go played. He was a little awkward, but he was strong and took the ball to the hoop like he meant it. Wortham had a nice game, but he was a senior and Go-Go was only a sophomore. Also, Go-Go was only eighteen, while Wortham was twenty-three.

I put the game behind me, more or less, and tried to concentrate a little more on the books. I was getting by in class okay, but I knew things weren't going so hot. Then the school paper, which came out twice a week, was sent around with a write-up about the game and I just about went crazy. They had two whole pages about the game with pictures and everything. I told myself that it didn't matter what they said about me, it was just important that the team won, but I found myself going through the stories looking for my name just the same. I finally found it in the next to last paragraph.

Lonnie Jackson, a product of New York's Harlem school yards, played the entire second half, mostly out of control, at guard. He combined poor shot selection with sloppy passing to reveal himself as a rank freshman. What he did do, however, was to crash both boards well and play good defense. Teufel might make a player out of him.

That ticked me off. I looked to see who had written it and saw that some guy named John Bowers had done it. I looked in the box score and saw that I had gone four for nine and had gotten three rebounds and one assist. I was down at practice the next day and couldn't get anything right. It was a funny feeling. You go out and play a basketball game and then you have to wait until the papers come out to see how you did. I knew

Leeds had read the paper, too, because he kept calling out for me to get myself under control.

We had a quiz in math and I messed it up pretty good. I knew as soon as I'd finished it that I didn't do well on it. So when Mr. Gunther asked me to stay for a while after class one day, I knew what it was all about.

"Did you take any math in high school?" he asked.

"Yeah, but I didn't do too well in it," I said.

"I don't understand what you were thinking about when you took this quiz," he said. "Because you didn't get a single problem right. Do you understand the work?"

"Some of it," I said.

"Look, Jackson, I give a quiz around this time of the year not to find out what you know but to find out who's doing the work I assign and who's listening in class. This is the easiest part of the year. If you have trouble with this, there's no way you're going to pass this course unless you really turn yourself around. Now, I'm not going to spend a lot of time on you. You either have to get yourself straightened up or take the consequences. Do you understand me?"

I said I did and then left. I knew what the dude was talking about, and I had told myself that I was really going to get down with the math. But the truth was, I didn't know a thing about the math. What he was saying just didn't make any sense to me at all. I copied the stuff down that he put on the board and it could have been Russian or something. I didn't even know how to start thinking about it. Teufel had said that if we ran into trouble with any of our courses, we should talk to him about it. I didn't want to talk to him about it, though. I hadn't run into trouble, I had run into a brick wall.

The St. Louis game had been exciting because it was my first college game. During the week after the game one of the redshirts dropped from the team and became a manager and two were put on the nontraveling team along with Sly. A lot of people didn't go for Sly. I think it was because he acted so black. I had never seen a white guy like him before in my life. He walked black and talked black, and at times I even thought he looked a little black. He was a good ballplayer, too, but I could tell that Teufel didn't like him that much and Leeds hated him.

When I found out that me, Colin, and Juice had made the traveling squad, I wanted to finesse it off like it was no big deal, but I had to smile. Later, when I saw Sherry in front of the library with some of her white friends and this doofus-looking brother, I had everything under control.

"Hey, baby." I spoke to her as I walked up to them. "Guess what Leeds ran down on me?"

"What?" she asked, looking like something good to eat.

"That they had been thinking about leaving me off the traveling team," I said.

"They aren't, are they?" she asked.

"You know better than that," I said. "I didn't come all the way out here to be watching games on television."

Then I just bopped away, real cool-like. I know she had to go for it because I dug it so much, I could hardly walk straight.

At home we had maroon uniforms with white trim and white warm-up suits with maroon trim. They were really nice. For the away games it was just the opposite, the playing uniforms were white with maroon trim. Our next game would be the first conference game and the first away game. We were playing at Missouri and the team flew with the cheerleaders, coaches, and press people. Students who wanted to go to the game took their cars or buses. We stayed at a motel on the edge of the city and it was really like big-time ball. I mean, if the NBA was fancier, it must have been something else.

The hometown provided buses for us to get from the motel to the gym we were playing in. It looked big from the outside and we had to take elevators to get to the locker rooms. But when we changed into our uniforms and went through this long hallway onto the gym floor, it was something else. They had a band that was twice as big as ours, and as soon as we got onto the floor, they started playing their school song.

I looked up and there must have been twenty thousand people in the gym. Their cheerleaders, dressed in pale blue, gave us a halfhearted cheer as we came onto the floor. Our cheerleaders were in front of our bench and they were going crazy. I had seen most of them around Orly Hall and they were okay at the St. Louis game, but they were really doing their thing on the road. This was a league game, and it was, as Teufel kept saying, big-time college basketball. My stomach tightened up.

I was watching the game from the bench. The first half of the game was close. Teufel said we were supposed to beat these guys but they were playing us hard. Larson couldn't get his stuff off at all. They had this brother on the floor who was all over him. Whenever they took him out, they brought in this other brother who was slow but was beating Larson to death. They played a two-one-two zone, which kept us away from the basket, but Hauser was hitting pretty good from the outside and we were up by two at the half. In the locker room Teufel got on Wortham's case pretty hard.

"The trouble is you're not making anything happen under the basket," Teufel shouted at Wortham from across the locker room. "Anybody can stand like a statue and wait for the ball to fall into his lap. You've got to make something happen! If you don't feel well, take yourself out of the game. They haven't got one man with three fouls and they haven't got one man who looks tired out there, so it's going to be a long second half."

"They foulin' plenty." Wortham had a towel over his head and his voice came from beneath it. "Referees just ain't calling them, that's all."

"The refs are calling the game okay," Leeds said. "They're letting you play ball instead of making it a foul-shooting contest, only it don't seem like you want to play any ball."

When I played ball back in Harlem, things were usually pretty cool in the locker room at half time if you were even or ahead. But we were winning and things were really tense. Wortham was playing okay, but okay wasn't good enough in college ball. When it was time to go back out on the floor, my hands were sweating. It was the first time in my life that I felt I had to win because someone else said so.

They jumped out in front before we could get back into the game, going up by five. Hauser got us back to within three with a short jumper, then stole the ball, but Wortham got called for standing in the lane three seconds and they got the ball back. Teufel turned red and threw a towel down on the bench. When we got the ball back, down by five again, Teufel called a time-out and put Go-Go in the game in Wortham's place.

There are dudes who are strong, and some who are strong and quick, and others who have shots that you can't seem to stop. There's also another kind of dude who has a feel for what's going on in the game that's different from anybody else's feel. Sometimes, when my game is on, I get a sense that I'm magical, that I can float through the air and reach out from anyplace on the floor and just stuff the ball through the hoop. When Go-Go went in, something like that happened.

He came down the floor the first time and moved into the center, near the foul line. Hauser threw the ball in to him and Go-Go turned, his body leaning into the guy holding him, and released the ball to Larson, who was cutting underneath. How he knew Larson would be at that exact spot, I don't know, but it was a beautiful play, so smooth that it didn't look at all spectacular. The second time down Hauser shot off a screen and Go-Go pushed in the rebound.

Neil's man started double-teaming Go-Go, and Teufel took him out and put me in, telling me to keep my man off Go-Go. I was anxious to get in. The first time I got my hands on the ball was on a break. Go-Go was trailing and Larson was headed down the other side of the floor. I could feel Go-Go's presence behind me and I went up high, faked a jumper, and laid it off to the big man cutting past me. He put it up softly against the backboard and we were suddenly tied.

For the next two minutes we played as if we were one person. For two minutes it was what basketball is all about, muscles working, bodies barely touching other bodies, passes just getting past straining fingertips to your man. We were living fast and strong and just beyond the reach of the rest of the world. Their coach called time out, and it ended. It wouldn't be that way again in that game.

We outmuscled them for most of the remainder to stay a little ahead. Then Larson came back in, got hot, and put the game away.

In the dressing room we felt pretty good. It's always good to win, you can talk about how good you did this and how good you did that instead of talking about who blew the game.

"Hey, Jackson." Leeds was standing near the locker where Skip was dressing. "On the play where you made the tap—you remember that play?"

"Yeah," I said. "I caught the cat trying to overplay me and hooked him with my elbow."

"And where the hell were you supposed to be for that play?" Leeds asked. "You didn't see Hauser hold up two fingers?"

I had seen Hauser hold up the two fingers. I was supposed to move through the low post, giving Go-Go the option of turning and shooting or turning and passing off to me. But when he got the ball I had forgotten.

"When are you going to learn the plays?" someone asked.

I looked up and there was this guy standing there with a tape recorder. "Who are you?" I asked.

"I'm Bowers, John Bowers," he said, as if that was supposed to mean something great. "I'm with the *Eagle.*"

"Yeah," I said. I turned and started putting on my clothes.

"Is that the way they play ball in Harlem?" Bowers asked. "You do what you want to?"

"No, man, that's not how they play ball," I said. "But I'm going to show you how they punch people in the mouth in just about one minute."

"Yeah, sure thing, fellow," Bowers said. I watched as he walked away. I figured that would be in the school paper the next time it came out.

We got back to Orly Hall and there were pizzas and Cokes waiting for us. They were from the Fat Man's place; and he was right, his pizzas were good. We ran down the game among ourselves. Teufel had taken off and everybody was talking as if Larson had won it by himself. I thought that Hauser had controlled the game for us.

"Go-Go played a good game, too," Larson said. "He took charge of the boards like he owned them when he was in."

"We've got to build around him," Leeds said. "By the end of the season we'll probably have to rely on him more and more."

I looked over at Wortham and he was looking away. It wasn't right for Leeds to talk him down like that, because good as Go-Go was, he still couldn't carry the team at center like Wortham could when his game was together. The most important thing, though, was why Wortham didn't speak on it.

After everybody had left, I went on up to the room. Colin was reading the Bible, which he did every night. I asked him if he wanted a Coke and he said he did. The Coke machine on our floor was empty and I went down to the day room. Neil was there.

"Hey, nice game," I said. I must have said that to everybody on the team at least twice, that's how excited I was.

"Yeah, man, it was okay," Neil said. "I see the coach likes you."

"Why you say that?"

"He put you in instead of Jake. Jake was always the man to go in at forward."

"Leeds don't like me," I said. "He had his little say when the game was over about how I blew a play."

"He always has something to say," Neil said. "I'll see you at practice."

"Hey, wait a minute," I called to Neil as he headed for the stairway. "What's this thing with Bobby? His game is better than Go-Go's but the way it looks . . . you know, they seem to be building Go-Go up so much."

"Between you and me?"

"Yeah," I said, "go on."

"Bobby's got a drinking problem," Neil said. "You see how late he comes to practice sometimes?"

"Yeah."

"You can't be bringing down the team by boozing it up," Neil said. "Anyway, he can't play his best game when he's tearing up his body."

"What did you say to him?" I asked.

"I didn't say anything to him," Neil said. "He knows what he's doing."

I didn't know Wortham that tough. He seemed to go his own way and didn't have no whole lot to say to anybody. Still, I couldn't figure out why Neil didn't say anything to him if he knew what was going down. I figured I'd speak to him if I had the chance. I didn't know what I could say to him, but at least I'd pull his coat that I heard about it.

When the school paper came out I was surprised that Bowers hadn't put anything in it about our little run-in. All it said about me was that I played a few "productive" minutes. I didn't know what that meant, exactly, but I figured nobody else did either, so I didn't think about it anymore.

6

"Yo! Lonnie, wake up!"

I shook my head, trying to clear the cobwebs away. I pushed myself away from the smell of stale beer and tried to figure out who was shaking me.

"Yo! Lonnie! C'mon, man, wake up!"

It was Sly. The lights were on and Sly was dressed. Colin was behind Sly, and he looked like he had hurt his hand or something and was trying to put a bandage on it.

"What's going on?" I asked. "What time is it, anyway?"

"Dig it, you got to get dressed and come downtown

with us," Sly said, pulling the cover off me. "Juice is jammed up in town."

"What you mean, jammed up?" I saw the clock. It read either two thirty or three thirty, I wasn't sure.

"Ain't got no time for explanations right now," Sly said. "Either you with us or you against us."

"You in a fight?"

"No, man, c'mon, we got to get my man out this jam."

"You talk to me real fast and real straight while I'm getting my clothes on," I said. "If I don't hear nothing, I ain't going no place."

"Look, Juice is in the music store in town," Colin said. "He can't get out."

"How come?"

"We were counting the jelly beans," Colin said over Sly's shoulders. "Sly figured we'd get in and count the jelly beans at night. We got in but Juice couldn't get out."

"You out."

"Yeah, but Juice ain't," Sly said. "Look, man, you're wasting time and the brother needs help."

I tied my sneakers and we started off. I took a look at Colin's hand and it looked like just a scrape. I was still only half awake when we got out in front of Orly Hall, but the damp night air shocked me back to my senses. If Colin hadn't been going along with the thing, I would have stayed in bed. We got out front and then me and Colin followed behind Sly around to the side of the building, where a cab was waiting. I got in and Colin got in beside me and then Sly got in the front in the driver's seat.

"Sly, what you doing driving?" I said.

"Somebody got to drive," he said.

"Where the driver?"

"He lent me the cab," Sly said.

"Hey, man, what's going on here?"

"We went down to the music store," Colin said, "and hung around trying to count the jelly beans in the jar."

"There must have been twenty people there counting them beans," Sly said. "Some of them had slide rules, calculators, the whole nine yards."

"So Sly figured we could slip into the store over the transom when the place closed, then count the jelly beans."

"You went along with that?" I looked at Colin and he shrugged.

"Hey, it's just as fair as using them slide rules," Sly said.

"Look where you driving, man," I told him.

"So we sat down and we counted all the beans," Colin said. "But then we started to leave and we found that the door had one of those double locks. Once the door is locked you had to have a key to get out."

"Yeah?"

"So we went back over the transom," Colin said. "Only the way the transom is built, it's easy to get into and hard to get out of. Juice couldn't make it."

"Crap!"

"And there are gates at the window, so we can't even break a window and get him out," Sly said.

"So what you come and get me for?" I asked. "He's the sap, let him take the rap."

"Sly has another idea," Colin said.

"Look, all we got to do is get somebody in who can give Juice a boost and hold him up while he wriggles through the transom, see," Sly said. "And you can get in and out easy."

"Hold time, how come *I* got to get in and out easy? I wasn't in this mess in the first place."

" 'Cause Colin could hardly get out himself the first time and now he's got a hurt hand," Sly said. "I'd go in myself but the reason somebody got to go in is to give Juice a boost and I ain't strong enough to be boosting that big brother. That only leaves you, my man. If you got the heart, you got the part."

We got to town and Sly parked the cab in an alley. I asked him why he parked in the alley and he said that the guy he borrowed the cab from didn't want it on the street. Yeah. Sure.

It was a sparrow trip. There was my man Juice in the store, behind bars, looking like a stone convict. The guy looked pitiful. I surveyed the situation carefully and quickly figured out the best thing to do.

"I'm going back to the dorm."

"Hey, we can't let Juice go down the tubes," Sly said.

"Look, if I can get in there, and I'm not sure I can, what happens if the cops come along? Bam! They got my butt for breaking and entering. Bam! They got Juice for breaking and entering. This is your idea, you go in."

"He's right," Colin said. "It was your idea."

We went across the street and pretended to look into some windows of a bookstore until one of the town's two patrol cars passed. Then we went over to the music store and boosted Sly up through the transom. He tried to lift Juice up so that he could get out of the transom but he couldn't make it. He just wasn't strong enough. I could see the clock in the church tower off the square. It was four thirty. It would be daylight soon and the way I figured it, Juice could be in a world of trouble. I had to help him.

I told Colin to give me a hand up and went over and into the store. My heart was beating as fast as it could. Me and Sly made a step with our hands for Juice and he tried again. Soon as I saw him go up I saw that there was no way he was going to make it.

"How did you get in that little space?" I asked.

"It wasn't easy," Juice said. "I got myself all skinned up getting in."

We sat there and looked at the transom for a while longer while we were waiting for the patrol car to pass again, then we tried to get Juice up again. He pushed and grunted a little, but it wasn't any use. He couldn't get out. I looked out at Colin and shook my head.

The only thing to do at that point, I figured, was to split. The thing was mean, but there wasn't any use for all of us to take the rap.

"I guess y'all going to leave me," Juice said.

"I can't see what else we can do," I said. I felt sorry for the brother but it looked hopeless. "If we try to bust out of here, the only thing we're going to do is set off an alarm or something, cause a lot of damage, and get into more trouble. Hey, maybe you could hide behind something and run out when the store opens."

The thought of Juice hiding behind a pole or something when the owner came in cracked me up and I had to smile a little. I turned away from Juice but he caught me and looked even sadder. Then I looked up and saw Colin coming through the transom. He got in with a little effort just as the patrol car came down the street. We all held our breaths as the patrol car stopped in front of the music store, then moved on. I looked over to where Colin was crouched down near a snare drum and saw he was holding a stick.

"What are you going to do with that?" I asked. "I ain't breaking no window in here."

"Look around for a hammer and nails," Colin said. "I've got an idea."

We looked around for a hammer and nails as Colin laid the plan out. We found a tool box in the back. Then Sly and Colin worked on the transom while me and Juice set things up.

We watched for the clock down the street, which we could see reflected off a mirror that the guy had on a shelf. The store was supposed to open at nine o'clock. We waited until eight forty-five. There were a lot of people walking past the shop, going to work, walking dogs, and whatnot. There were some students going past too. A few had already stopped and were looking at the jelly beans in the jar in the window when we started.

Sly wasn't bad on drums. Colin had given Juice a xylophone and showed him what notes to beat on. I had a cowbell and a little stick I was hitting it with, and Colin was playing a guitar. He had hooked it up to an amplifier and it just about drowned out the rest of us, thank God.

We had a small crowd out in front of the place by the time the owner got to the store. We could see him standing out front and looking at his store like he didn't know whether to spit or go blind. We had put the lights on so the students could see us and some of them were clapping along with us and a few were even dancing.

The store owner ran around to the side door, saw that it was locked, shrugged, and started opening the gates. A policeman came by and he stopped him and pointed to us. We couldn't hear what they were saying, but I'm sure the policeman was asking him how we got in, because he shrugged again. Then he and the policeman went around to the side door and saw that it was still locked. Every time they looked in at us we'd smile and keep on playing. The policeman came in the front door with the store owner and a lot of kids. The kids started dancing around us and one guy picked up some clave sticks and started playing them. The policeman went to the side door with the owner but kept an eye on us. They checked the door again and then checked the transom, but Colin and Sly had nailed the stick across the inside so it couldn't be opened, at least not enough to let anyone in. Colin had figured from the dirt on the transom that the store owner hadn't bothered with it for years and wouldn't remember if he had put the stick there or not.

"Okay, okay, you guys!" The policeman raised both hands and we stopped playing. Some of the girls that had come in with the policeman and the owner kept dancing until the policeman gave them a look. "How did you guys get in here?"

"It's a military secret," Colin said. "The university is working on a research project designed to put people through walls."

"Don't play grab-ass with me, punk!" The policeman, a big dude with ears that came down to the middle of his jaws, stuck his face into Colin's.

The crowd started booing and the policeman looked like he wanted to punch someone.

"You gonna press charges against these clowns?" the policeman asked, looking at us.

"Nooo!!" The people in the store all called out at once.

"I guess not," the store owner said, looking around and not seeing any damage.

It took us another ten minutes, after we had all given our names to the policeman in case anything was missing, before we could go. The store owner thought it was some kind of a college joke or something. Then the policeman gave us ten minutes to get out of the store and out of town.

"Where you guys going?" Sly asked as me, Colin, and Juice headed for the bus stop.

"Back to campus," Juice said. "You think that cop wasn't serious?"

"C'mon, man," Sly said. "We'll take the cab, might as well go back in style."

We told Sly what he could do with his cab, and when he said it wouldn't fit we all volunteered to break it down into pieces that would.

We had just got back to the dorm when the Fat Man called and asked if I wanted to coach a game between the mill guys and the post office team he had talked about before.

"Larson says he's tied up," the Fat Man said. He had a voice that sounded as if it was coming out of his chest. "There's fifty bucks in it for you if you want it."

I said okay. What I wanted was to take Sherry out, and I needed the fifty. I remembered what Cal had said about easy money. I wasn't going to get the money for nothing, after all. I *was* working for it.

I sat around with Colin for a while after I had spoken to the Fat Man, and he asked me if there was anything wrong, and I told him no.

"I just get down sometimes," I said.

"You call home recently?" he asked.

"What are you, now?" I asked. "My moms away from home?"

"Yeah," Colin said. "Why don't you call home?"

It was funny for him to say that and it took me by surprise. He didn't care about the little names I was laying on him if he could help me. I hadn't really thought about us being that tight, but I guess we were, or at least we were heading in that direction.

I decided to make the call from the library. I felt good as I started out, but as I got near the library I got this funny feeling in my stomach. I started thinking of things I was going to say and I kept changing them in my mind. It didn't make any sense to me that I was nervous about calling my own mother. I knew there were things she would want to hear, about how good I was getting on and how much I was getting out of college, things like that. But I wasn't sure if I could make her understand how I was feeling.

It wasn't just that things were hard, because they weren't really. I had hustled food from the supermarket when I was ten. There had been a time, when my moms was sick, that I had to fight my way through the junkies to get to the drugstore and get her prescription filled, and then fight my way past them again to keep it. I could take hard, I had learned to handle it. This was different. I had been man enough to struggle and get over in Harlem; in Montclare I was struggling just to let people know I was for real.

"Hey, Mom, what's happening?"

"Lonnie? Is that you, baby? Oh, I'm so glad to hear you. How you doing out there?"

"I'm doing just fine," I said. "I had to make some adjustments, but things are working out. And how about you? How've you been?"

"Pretty good. I've been doing pretty good," she said.

"I think you'd like it out here," I said. "All those open spaces you used to talk so much about. Maybe you can come out one day."

"I don't know. . . ." Her voice kind of died out a little. "Now that you in college and everything, I'm not sure if I know how to talk to you. You should hear yourself, soundin' so proper and everything. You must be doin' good at that school."

"Doing okay," I said. "It sure doesn't seem like I've been away three months."

"It'll be three months this coming Saturday," she said. "You like it out there?"

"It's a lot different than being home," I said. "It's nice."

"You got a new girlfriend?"

"Well, I met this girl," I said, "but Sherry and I aren't really serious."

"She's going to the college, too?"

"Yeah, she's in some of my classes."

"Lonnie, you sure sound good," Mom said. "I can't wait to see somebody and tell them how good you're soundin'."

We talked for a while longer and I felt sorry I had to say good-bye to her. I was really surprised at how she sounded. I had never thought about how we talked in Harlem before, and wondered how I sounded. I didn't get around to telling her that I missed her, or that I missed Harlem either. That kind of thing was still hard for me to say. I didn't tell her that I hadn't made many friends, or that I didn't think many of the people at Montclare liked me. No use in getting her worried.

The game between the mill guys and the post office dudes was jive. Pure and simple. The mill guys didn't play as well as they did against us, but they didn't have to, either. The post office guys played well for the first five minutes and even went ahead a little, but they were out of shape. By the end of the first twenty-minute half they were huffing and puffing around the court. The mill guys ate them up. I couldn't see anybody betting on the game, but the Fat Man went around to some guys and it looked like he was collecting money.

After the game the mill guys were all happy, as if they had really done something. They wanted to talk the game, to act like ballplayers. It took forever to get away from them. They even wanted me to go have some beer with them. I said I couldn't because I was in training. They said they understood that and thanked me for coaching. Yeah.

The Fat Man gave me the money and I put it in my pocket without counting it.

"That post office team was crap," the Fat Man said. "A bunch of stiffs."

"Somebody must have thought they were okay," I said. "If there was money on them."

"Nah, it ain't the game." The Fat Man drove with one hand. He had two big rings on his hand. "It's the action. Guys like to bet, 'cause they get a chance to be winners. You don't know about that, see, because you're a winner already or they wouldn't have you playing ball for Montclare. The average guy, though, he don't win nothing in his life. When he was a kid, like you, he didn't make the teams 'cause he wasn't good enough. When he got older he couldn't play anything either. Chances are he's either not married or he's got some dame that's breaking his chops. His boss kicks his butt, his telephone bills kick his butt, everything kicks his butt. But if he bets, he can be a winner."

"Or a loser," I said.

"That don't matter," the Fat Man said. He looked over at me as if I had said something wrong. "It doesn't matter if you lose as long as you get to win sometime, college boy."

The Fat Man dropped me off at the campus and said he'd see me around. Sometimes I thought he liked me and sometimes, like when he said "college boy" just before dropping me off, I felt he didn't. I didn't think it was because I'm black, because I didn't feel he liked Larson that much either. It might have had something to do with us going to college, I wasn't sure. But it was funny, in a way, getting something else in my life that people didn't like me for.

Back in Harlem we used to talk about going to college a lot. Most of the guys never made it, and in our hearts we didn't have much faith in our actual going, but we talked about it all the same. You could hang out on the streets and look around you and see other dudes hanging out, guys that should have been working or going to college or something. Instead they were just there, waiting for something to happen, while the days piled up on them and pushed them down. After a while they were as much a part of the street itself as the lampposts and the fire hydrants. I could see this just the same as the others, but I kept hoping that something different would happen to me. Nothing had until Cal came along.

Cal had played college ball and then went on to the NBA. He did okay there until he got in with some gamblers and started shaving points. The gamblers would decide that one team should beat the others by, say, five points. That five points would be the "spread." Then they would pay a player, someone like Cal, to keep the winning total down to four points so they could collect their bets. Cal went for it, got caught, and was kicked out of the NBA.

After that he went downhill until when I met him he was a wino, just a step up from sleeping in the streets. Someone from the community center knew him and arranged to have him coach our team in a Coaches

Tournament. It was in the Coaches Tournament that Cal taught me a lot about the game and about myself. He got me to the point where I could control my game and myself enough for someone like Teufel to offer me a scholarship out to Montclare.

I went into the library and counted the money. It was all there, fifty bucks. I had made fifty bucks for just standing on the sideline watching the mill guys play against—what had the Fat Man called them?—a bunch of stiffs. I thought back to Cal and all the trouble he had got himself into with gamblers in the NBA. It had blown his whole career. What would he have said if he saw me sitting in the library counting the money?

"The Fat Man is buying," he would have said. "What are you selling?"

I told myself that I wasn't selling anything.

7

One thing that Sherry got me into was movies. At first I thought it was stupid to go see an old movie and then sit around and talk about it all day like it was something great. I went along with it because that's what she wanted mostly to do when we went out. I figured she thought we weren't going to get into anything too heavy in a movie, and she was right. But after a while I began to dig the movies, too. Once she began to talk about them, you could see a lot more things in them.

When I picked her up after coaching the game for the Fat Man, she was looking great. She wore this short white dress with a pleated bottom and white shoes. When she sat down and that dress fell across those coffee-brown thighs, my eyes damn near got the hic-cups from checking her out. Instead of regular ear-rings she had earrings made of feathers that curled along her cheek, and I could have sworn they were pointing right toward her lips.

This movie wasn't much, something about what life was going to be like in the future. Everything was supposed to be hard. People were taking pills to get high, taking pills to get happy, taking pills to eat, the whole bit. There weren't any black people in the pic-ture. I figured that whoever made the flick didn't fig-ure we'd be around in the future.

I still wasn't sure about Sherry. I wanted to put my arm around her, but I didn't know if she wanted me to or not. It was a funny thing, because if we had been in Harlem, I'd put my arm around her and wouldn't think nothing of it. Only this was her turf. Even if she wasn't white, it was still her turf somehow. I sat through half the flick being bored and then I put my arm around her to see what she would do. She squeezed my hand and put it on her stomach. All right!

So then I kissed the mama on her ear. She turned up to me and laid this heavy kiss on me with about as much tongue action as I could handle. I didn't see the rest of the flick. It was true-love time in the balcony. She was twisting around in her seat and kissing and holding and everything else. She was letting her hands wander around my body in ways that were driving me crazy and I just went along for the ride.

By the time the movie was over and the lights came on I was breathing as if I had just run the hundred-yard dash about six times in a row. I waited while Sherry went into the ladies' room to get herself together. When she came out she was just about glowing, she looked that good. I felt like dragging her off into the bushes or something. My cave man thing was definitely coming out and I figured she was ready for it.

I had enough bread for a motel and I guessed that was the play. I hadn't seen any motels around but I thought that I could find one in the Yellow Pages.

"I'm exhausted," Sherry said, putting her arm around my waist. "I think when I get back to the dorm I'm going to sleep for twenty-four hours straight."

"If you're that tired," I whispered into her ear, "maybe we can find some place for you to lay down."

"The only place I'm lying down is in my bed," she said. "You know what time I got up this morning? I had to wash just about everything I owned."

"Your roomie out tonight?"

"Linda? I don't think so," Sherry said. "Why?"

"I thought we could spend the night together," I said, trying to make my voice sound as sexy as I could.

"Is that what they do where you come from?" Sherry pulled away from me. "You take a girl to a movie and then she has to pay you with sex? Is that what they do where you come from?"

I was trying to think of a comeback when she turned and walked away. Some of the other people from the movie were standing around and some were looking at me. I watched Sherry hop into one of the cabs parked outside the theater and in a moment she was gone.

I felt like a fool, like a jackass. I felt like running after her and punching her out. I was mad and hurt at the same time. I didn't know a thing about Sherry, I was sure. But I was even more sure that she didn't know a thing about Lonnie Jackson!

"Look." Larson and I were playing against each other at practice. He was guarding me at the low post and talking into my ear. "You know I like the Fat Man, he's got a thousand on us to win our next game, so you'd better hustle your ass if you want any free pizza, bright eyes."

I ignored Larson, took a pass from Hauser, and went up with a turnaround jumper that he slapped away.

"You should have been looking for somebody cutting!" Leeds said, after blowing his whistle. "I want you to count how many guys you have playing with you, Mr. Jackson. Go ahead, count 'em."

"Four guys," I said.

"I don't want you to tell me how many guys from memory, Jackson." Leeds jumped up into my face. "I told you to count 'em!"

I walked off the floor and went on into the locker room. Leeds didn't get on anybody else the way he got on me and I was sick and tired of it. I was sitting in the locker room for about a hot minute when Neil came in.

"Hey, man, what's wrong with you?" he asked, standing over me.

"What's wrong with Leeds?" I asked. "He's the one going crazy out there."

"He's not going crazy. You are." Neil took off his

sweat shirt. "You're the one that's making it bad for us out there."

"Bad for *who?*"

"For the brothers on the team, that's who," Neil said. "When I first came here I was the only brother on the team. The cat laid it down to me straight. He said that if I kept myself cool I could make it easier for any other brother to get a chance to play here. So, hey, I've been cool and you dudes got a chance to come to Montclare and get a piece of scholarship. Now you going to blow the whole thing, right? You going into your lame bag and making us all look bad, right?"

I couldn't believe I was hearing right. I looked up at the cat and saw that his face was all puffed up like I had said something bad about his mother or something.

"Look, Neil." I stood up so I could face the cat. "You go Tom for these suckers if you want, just leave me out the mess."

"You're a fool, man." Neil was looking at me and shaking his head. I wanted to go up side his head so bad I could feel it. "If you ain't a fool, you're going to go back down there and apologize to the man. Other than that you can kiss your scholarship bye-bye."

"I didn't come into the world with no scholarship," I said. "And I don't have to leave with none."

I showered and dressed. I was just leaving the locker room when the others started coming in. Nobody said anything to me except my roomies, they all showed tough. Even Leeds didn't say anything.

That afternoon I got a call to come over to Teufel's office. I figured that he was going to pussyfoot around the way Neil did and talk some trash about how I had to shape up. He didn't do much pussyfooting.

"You're suspended from the team for a week," he said as I walked into the room. "The next offense and you're off the team for good. I also expect you to apologize to each member of the team. If you don't want to do that, you can turn your uniform in. Now get out of here."

I went to the game the next day and sat up in the top seats. Kent State was in and they didn't look that tough. But they did have this dude named Junior Stephens on the team and he was bad. I had played against him in the Bronx about four or five times. He was good when I played against him but a little awkward. Now the cat had grown about five inches and smoothed out. He was playing against Wortham and was giving him a rough game. Larson had a bad first half and the team was down by twelve at the half, but I had the feeling that the guys were going to get themselves together. Things were just a little off. They put my man Colin in for a while and he hit two nice jumpers from the corner just before half time.

The second half started out just as I figured it would. Larson began to work his show. He took over the game for about five minutes. Then the whole game fell apart as Stephens took over the rebounding and started scoring on the inside. It looked as if Wortham had just run out of steam. They brought in Go-Go to replace Wortham but Kent State boxed him out on the boards and the refs called some jive fouls on him real quick and you could see him looking over at the bench to see what Leeds was going to say. We lost by a point in a game we should have walked away with.

I felt terrible. It was the first game we lost and for the first time I got the feeling that I was part of the team, even though I was sitting out the game.

The room was quiet when the guys came in. I had picked up some Cokes and passed them around. I wanted to ask them what happened but I was kind of ashamed to, because I felt it was my fault, or at least partially my fault. If I had been there I could have helped out with the rebounds.

"Bobby was half drunk," Sly said. "Teufel was going to start Go-Go but Wortham looked a little better after he had taken a shower."

"Before the game?"

"Yeah," Sly said. "I still thought we were going to win it in the second half but Wortham just kind of collapsed."

"They called some jive calls on Go-Go too," I said.

"No, that ain't what happened," Juice said. "You remember when they were fighting for that loose ball and they were on the floor?"

"Yeah."

"That 22 on their team hit Go-Go in his jewels."

"I thought he hurt his knee," I said.

"He didn't want to rub his balls in front of everybody," Sly said. "That 22 just kept beating on him and Neil wouldn't do anything about it. Hauser elbowed him in the side of his head but he didn't get a good shot at him."

"That 22's not even a regular," Colin said. "They

put him in to give that black forward a breather, but when he just beat on Go-Go and Neil wouldn't do anything about it, they left him in."

"What did Teufel say about Wortham?" I asked.

"He said something to him and then they went into his office after the game," Juice said.

I called Sherry later that night and asked if we could go out and she got on her high horse about she didn't come to college to party all the time and whatnot. I asked her what the movie was all about. She acted as if she had wanted to do more than party when we were in the flick. She came back with how sorry she was that she had even gone out with me, and that I didn't seem to understand anything.

Well, she was right about that. And it was for sure that I didn't understand where she was coming from. I hadn't thought about it a whole lot, but when I got into the college thing I picked up a dream along with the scholarship. I figured I would come out to Montclare and be a star and meet all kinds of super cool people. But the real deal was that everybody was looking at me to see what I could give up. Teufel and Leeds wanted me to help them win games but not be too out front when I did it, and God only knew what Sherry wanted. What I was pretty sure that she didn't want, what none of them wanted, was a street guy from Harlem.

Another thing I was thinking was that important as basketball was to me, it really wasn't that important to the rest of the world, no matter what it seemed like at times. I got to Montclare by playing ball, but if I ever got to the end of something good, I didn't think it was going to be ball.

8

I had been getting along pretty good with Eddie. His mother kept going on about how much she was amazed that he responded to me and everything and how good I was with kids. But Eddie was pretty good with people too. The first time I saw him after I got suspended from the team I was really uptight. I got the feeling that Teufel didn't care if I was on the team or not. Eddie hardly ever spoke, but when I stopped shooting with him and held the ball while I thought of what was going on with the team, he must have sensed something was wrong.

"You okay?" he asked. He had a funny way of turning his head sideways when he spoke.

I looked at him and he looked at me and then away. He was still shy, but he was worried about me, I could tell. I told him everything was going to be all right.

"I'm glad," he said. He didn't crack a smile. No teeth showing, no phony handshake, just a few words from the heart.

That was on a Tuesday. When I saw him that Thursday it was my turn to see that something was wrong.

When I got to the clinic, Eddie and his mother were already there. I thought I was late or something, but I wasn't. Eddie came into the gym, and when I started playing with him he responded right away. He played against me just like there was nothing wrong with him. He played too hard, going for the ball when he didn't even have a chance to get it, trying to force himself past me, that kind of thing. I figured maybe he needed to work off some energy so I let him play himself out.

We played for about an hour straight and the sweat was pouring off him. Then I set up some chairs for him to dribble around and he did that for a half hour until I made him stop.

"You playing some hard ball," I said.

"Can you play tomorrow?" he asked.

"I don't think I can come tomorrow, my man."

"Please!"

There was something in his face, I don't know what it was, but I didn't like it. It was like he was desperate to have me play with him right away. I looked over at his mother and she gave me this little weak smile. I thought for a minute, then remembered that I would be free about four o'clock.

"You get here about four, maybe four-fifteen?" I asked Eddie loud enough for his mother to hear me.

He turned to her and she nodded and started walking out.

Eddie was covered with sweat and I threw him a sweat jacket.

"Put this on, man, so you don't catch cold."

He was putting it on when he left.

"What's going down with Eddie?" I asked Ann when I had finished washing up.

"I don't know," she said. "Is he okay today? He looked a little upset."

"He played ball against me," I said. "He went the whole nine yards today."

"Maybe he's going through another phase," she said.

"I'm going to come over tomorrow and play with him for a while."

"That's nice," she said. "I think you really have a way with kids."

"Maybe I do," I said. "Anyway, I'll see you tomorrow."

The hardest thing I had to do was to go around apologizing to everyone. I got my roomies all together and they said to forget about it, like I thought they would. Then I got Go-Go, who was more embarrassed about it than me. I went all the way down the line, leaving Leeds and Hauser for last, because I knew they were going to give me some static. Finally, I got to Leeds and said I was sorry I gave him a hard time.

"You're sorry that you gave me a hard time and I'm

sorry that you didn't stay in Harlem," Leeds said. "I guess we're both sorry, huh?"

He spat on the floor in front of me and walked away. Beautiful. I only had Hauser to deal with.

Hauser was a sweet ballplayer. He could shoot, he was fast, and he could pass like a dream. The only thing wrong with him was that he was only about five ten. I played against him in practice and he could do a lot of things against me, he was that good, but he couldn't shoot over me. And because he couldn't shoot over me I could concentrate on his going around me. I couldn't stop his passes because he could pass with either hand and you couldn't tell from his eyes where he was going to pass. He was a good college ballplayer, but I didn't think he could ever make the pros.

He wasn't from the South, but you could tell he didn't like anybody that wasn't white. Sometimes he would make little cracks about Mexicans—there were a few of them on campus—or about some of the students from Korea and places like that. They were out-and-out racist kind of stuff and I told him about it one day. He asked me if it bothered me and I said it did. He said, "Well, isn't that a shame."

I saw him in the rec room at Orly Hall and laid my apology on him.

"Hey, man, the coach said I have to apologize to everybody on the team," I said. "So, you know, I'm sorry about what happened the other day."

"Yeah," he said, lining up a pool shot, "you're about as sorry as they come, bright eyes."

"My name is Jackson," I said. "You call me that."

"Right, bright eyes."

I wanted to punch him out bad, but I knew I'd just be walking around apologizing to everybody again, so I let it lay. I figured my day would come around.

We played a nonleague game against Grambling, an all-black team from Louisiana. Teufel started Go-Go at center and played Colin and Juice some in the first half. Juice didn't have a good game at all. He was big and strong but he wanted to play on the outside and Teufel wanted him to play inside. He didn't like being the muscle and you could tell. Colin wasn't as strong as Juice but they let him play anywhere he wanted. Wherever he played he looked good, and I figured that unless they got somebody else better, he would be starting in a year.

I didn't get into the game at all. I sat on the bench and cheered for the guys as they took Grambling easily. After the game Coach Teufel was to have dinner with the Grambling coach, and Larson drove them someplace off campus. I saw Larson later in Orly Hall and he said that one of the Grambling players was thinking about transferring to Montclare and Teufel was interested. They had a forward that looked pretty good, but the rest of their team wasn't that much. I told that to Larson.

"They scout for each other, too," Larson said. "Sometimes if Teufel sees a black ballplayer that he doesn't want, he'll pass him on to the guy at Grambling. And if he sees a white ballplayer, he'll scoop Teufel."

"I thought that Grambling was integrated," I said.

"They can't get the big players, black or white," Larson said. "That's what integration does for you."

"That right?"

"The Fat Man wanted to know why you weren't playing the other day," Larson said. "I told him that Leeds was messing over you."

"Oh, yeah," I said. "I bet he was ticked when he lost his bread. He really have a thousand on the game?"

"He did okay," Larson said.

"How could he do okay if he bet on us to win and we lost?" I asked.

"Hey, man, look." Larson rolled up his copy of *Sports Illustrated* and put it in his jacket pocket. "The Fat Man is smart money. Guys like that don't lose. He told me that he bet that we would win but that we wouldn't beat the spread. That way, even if we lose, he wins because we didn't beat the spread. That's smart money, man."

"Yeah, right," I said. Larson made me want to throw up.

It was the weekend and I found myself in the room wishing we had a television. Weekends at Montclare were garbage if we didn't have a game. Sometimes, if we had a game Monday or Tuesday, we'd have to practice on Sunday. It was better than doing nothing. Sherry was away at a track meet and there wasn't much for me to do in town. Colin never had any money, so we'd end up hanging out together sometimes. Sly and Juice would hang out in the city, but I didn't much go for it. Sometimes I'd play pickup games in the gym but that wasn't really cool, because it made me look like a basketball freak with nothing else to do. So when Colin came up with an idea I went for it.

"I'm going home," he said. "My sister is coming to pick me up tonight. Why don't you come with me?"

"How far is it?" I asked.

"Not far. My father's never seen a black guy, so I figure I'd bring you home and show him how one looks," Colin said.

"You kidding me, man?" I looked at Colin putting some things in his overnight bag. "You mean to tell me your father has *never* seen a black guy?"

"Are you kidding *me?*" Colin asked, laughing. "Can you really sit there and believe that anybody in the country has never seen a black person? You people in New York must have walls around the city."

"You know, you're the second person that's told me that," I said. "I always thought that New York was pretty hip."

"Hey, that's an idea," Colin said. "I'll take you home with me and then you can take me to Harlem."

"You got to be kidding. What would I do with you in Harlem?"

"Look, what else do you have to do this weekend?" Colin asked.

"Yeah, okay," I said. "Why not? When's your sister going to get here?"

"I figure she'll be here in about an hour or so," Colin said.

"How come you going home this weekend, anyway?" I asked.

"That's about the only thing you do with home, isn't it?" Colin asked. "Go back to it or leave it?"

Colin's sister looked a lot like him. She was tall, almost six feet, and had wide shoulders. She looked at me when Colin told her that I was coming home with them and shook her head, like she was agreeing with him.

"My name's Ruth," she said. "My father named the two girls from the Bible. My sister's name is Naomi. She's married and lives in Texas. My father had religion when he named us. Then he had Colin, took one look, and lost his religion."

She didn't smile when she told a joke. Her expression hardly ever changed. She wasn't bad-looking, not exactly good-looking either. She looked like the kind of woman who would be someplace waiting for you when you got back from wherever you'd been. Her face and hands, up close, looked as if she had been in the cold weather. Her knuckles were red.

She was driving an old Ford Fairlane that ran fairly nice. You could see that it had rusted a little near the rear right fender and that someone had painted over it with a brush.

"How are things?" Colin asked.

"The thyme did all right," Ruth said. "Everything else died."

"Pa thought he would try growing herbs instead of a regular food crop," Colin said. "Figured that even if it didn't do that well he could bring it in and market it himself. Seemed like a good idea."

"Good ideas don't grow in that sand any more than anything else," Ruth said.

"You think he should give it up and do something else?" I asked.

"I do," Ruth said. "I don't see any sense to throwing bad money after good. Colin sees some sense to it, but it's beyond me, it truly is."

"Pa's got to have something to do, something to believe in," Colin said.

"Even if it's a lie." Ruth looked at her brother sitting next to her in the front seat. "That's all that land's been since I can remember. A lie about what we're going to have when he dies."

Colin didn't say anything. He jammed his hands in his pocket, which made his shoulders looked hunched up somehow, and sank into a mood. I had seen him go into moods like that before, mostly when he got letters from home.

We drove straight through from the college to Cisne on a highway and then took a turnoff Ruth and Colin called a spur, to where they lived. It was almost dark when we reached the house. It didn't look bad. In fact, it was a nice house except that the porch was higher on one side than the other.

"We added the porch on after the house," Colin said as we walked across it. "The house had settled evenly but the porch settled lopsided."

Colin's mother opened the door. She was short, a little on the plump side, with a high forehead and dark hair that had streaks of red and gray in it.

"Hey, Mom, this is my roommate Lonnie." Colin's mother came up to his chest and she was hugging him around the waist so hard that I thought she was going to throw him over. She saw me and straightened up and wiped her hands off on her apron before reaching over to shake my hand.

"Mom always loved Colin more than she loved me," Ruth said. She was smiling. She loved Colin a lot, too, you could see that.

"I'm pleased to meet you, Mr. Lonnie." Colin's mother gave me a little half bow and looked over at Colin.

"I figured he could stay in Naomi's room," Colin answered. "Where Pa?"

"In the house trying to feel important. He said he wasn't going to come out and greet you because now that you're a college boy you might get a big head. He's going to feel like a right fool when he sees you brought along a real college boy for a guest."

"Wait a minute, now." Colin put his arm around his mother's shoulder as we headed for the house. "How come *he's* a real college boy and I'm not?"

"Oh, you know what I mean," his mother said, looking back at me. "You're just you, you know that."

Colin's father was where he got his height from. He was a good inch taller than Colin. He was thin on top, and wide shouldered, but he had a pot belly. His belly looked like it belonged to another person. So did his ears. His ears stuck out on both sides as if somebody had stuck them on his head to be funny.

"Pa, this is Lonnie Jackson. He's on the basketball team, too," Colin said. "He's from New York."

"New York City?"

"Yes, sir," I said.

"Well, you're probably the first person we've ever had in this house from New York City."

"Is not," Mrs. Young said. "We had that old gal that married the Thompson boy in here."

"She had just been to New York, Mama," Ruth said. "She wasn't *from* New York. Lonnie was born and raised in New York."

"New York isn't the only place in the world, is it, young fellow?"

"No, sir."

"But I bet it sure is some place, from what we hear down here," Mr. Young said. "I bet it sure is some place."

We had dinner, which was really good. Colin's mother had made buttermilk cornbread, roasted pork strips in gravy, string beans, rice, and spinach.

"When Colin was little, he wanted to have spinach every day because he thought he was going to be as strong as . . . as . . ." She made a little fluttering movement with her hand.

"Popeye," Ruth said.

"That's right," Mrs. Young said.

I didn't think Mrs. Young was comfortable around me. Whatever she did she kept looking over at me like she expected me to be doing something strange.

After dinner Mr. Young took me around to show me the place. You could see that he was proud of it. The place was big, or at least it was big as far as I was concerned. They had a barn with two cows in it and a small pony they said was almost twelve years old.

"I used to ride him around when I was a kid," Colin said. "And I used to change his name about once a month, which always made Ruth and Naomi mad. They would call him Tony, after some cowboy horse, but I would change his name to Pee-wee, or Fast Billy, things like that. He'd come to me no matter what I'd call him but he'd never come to them. That used to get them both ticked off."

"One day, when I meet my maker," Mr. Young said, "Colin's going to have to find something to do with this place. I don't care what he does with it, either. He can cement the whole thing over and make a parking lot out of it, I don't care."

"Ruth said the thyme came up nice," Colin said.

"It came up okay," Mr. Young said. "Talked to a fellow about some jars—you know, drying it out and putting it up in jars. He said I couldn't do it as cheap as they had down in the supermarket. You know what I asked him? You know what I asked him?"

"What did you ask him, Pa?"

"I asked him if I looked like a fool to him," Mr. Young said. "That's what I asked him. I told him that I knew I couldn't produce it as cheap as the supermarket. And the supermarket couldn't produce it as fresh as I could, either."

"What did he say to that?" I asked.

"What could he say?" Mr. Young said. "There wasn't anything left to say after that."

I couldn't sleep for two cents the first night. It wasn't the quiet, I had gotten used to that about a week after I reached Montclare. I think it was just the excitement of being there. Colin's mother jumping around behind him was funny in a way, and I wondered if she had ever worked the way my mother had. She didn't look the type. His father looked like a hard-working man, though. I could see where somebody could get attached to a piece of land. It was yours, like a car was yours, or like a dollar was yours, but it was more than that. You worked it and it was your job, it was what you owned, where you lived, and what you had to leave to your kids. It was more like your whole life. I could see that a man could get attached to a piece of land.

The first day we were there was Saturday, and Colin got me up before daybreak to help him with the chores. There were a thousand things to do. We went out and fed the cow and he showed me how you were supposed to milk the things, but I thought it looked a little freaky messing with a cow's private parts so I didn't try it. Then we went and took some rocks and burlap off a piece of land which they had put a lot of fertilizer on. Colin ran his fingers through it and picked some of it up.

"How it look?" I asked.

"It'll take another thirty years before this land is worth anything," he said. "In a way I'm glad that it's as dead as it is. If it wasn't, if it showed a little more life, I'd have been stuck going to agricultural college."

"Your father thinks it's okay," I said.

"He wanted me to go to agricultural college, but I didn't," Colin said. "If the land was halfway decent, I would have anyway."

We worked until nine and then we had breakfast. Later we went back into the fields and helped his father turn over some land he was thinking about planting some more herbs in.

"Hey, man, who does all this when you're not here?" I asked.

"Mom and Ruth and Dad all pitch in," Colin said. "But since we got us a New York City boy here, Mom and Ruth are in the house acting like ladies."

"I don't think your mother likes the idea of me being here too much," I said.

"She's scared to death of you," Colin said. "She came into my room last night to talk and she told me that."

Colin had showed me how to till with a little portable machine in between the fences his father had built for the animals he was going to buy one day. I cut the power and wiped my brow off with my shirtsleeve.

"Told you to tie that handkerchief around your head," Colin said. "This sun'll kill you faster than bad liquor."

"How come she's scared of me?" I asked. "Because I'm black?"

"Nope, because you go to college. She thinks she's going to open her mouth and say something stupid and then the whole family is just going to be embarrassed. She's always been like that. She doesn't read too well."

"That right?"

"That's right," Colin said.

I went to church with them on Sunday and smiled at everybody staring at me. I was the only person in the church that wasn't white. When the word got around that I was one of Colin's basketball teammates, some of the younger kids came up and asked me if I could dunk. When I said yes, they wanted me to go in the back of the church where they had a basket set up and show them, but their parents dragged them off. The truth was, I wanted to go back there and dunk for them.

The rest of the day went well. Colin and I helped his father fix the door to the storm cellar. The old man liked to have his son working with him, you could see the pride in his face. Some of Colin's younger friends came around, some he had played ball with in high school. They were all big, strong-looking dudes, the kind that worked with their hands. We sat around and talked and they didn't seem much different from Colin. Colin's mother made a pie and between Colin, me, and two of his friends, we ate the whole thing. When it was finally time to leave I didn't want to go.

Colin's mother told him that she had some forms for him to look at and took him back into the house just before we were ready to get into the car. The sun had just gone down, and off in the distance there was an even band of orange sky.

"You know, she doesn't have any papers in there for him to look at before he goes," Ruth said. She had changed from a dress into gray slacks and a pink sweater and was looking kind of good. Colin's father was in the house shining his church shoes. "She's just shamed of hugging him so much in front of you."

"How do you like living out here?" I asked as we waited for Colin.

"I don't like it that much," Ruth said.

"Why not? It looks pretty nice to me," I said. "You know, back in Harlem we used to see this as the perfect kind of life. I mean, it looks like there's some work involved with it, but it's nice."

"I want something more," Ruth said, leaning against the fender of the car. "I want to be all excited about something, have people excited about me for some reason—you know, that kind of thing. Sometimes when I read about the big cities and hear about the crime in them I start thinking about what I would do to protect myself. I'd have all these daydreams about taking karate lessons or getting a derringer, silly stuff like that. And that'd be the best part of my whole day."

"So what are you going to do?" I asked.

"Sit around and wait for Daddy to die, so I'll have to make a decision, I guess," Ruth said. "Here comes your star forward. Is he really any good?"

"He's real good," I said.

"I always knew he would be," she said. "I really did."

9

The day after I got back I got a call to go to the administration office. When I got there a clerk told me that I had to sign some papers. She found them and handed them to me and told me where to sign.

"What's this mean?" I asked. I could see it was some kind of form about a change in curriculum but I couldn't figure out just what it was.

The girl took the paper and looked it over.

"Oh, you're dropping math," she said. "That's what it says here. Did you apply to drop math?"

"Oh, yeah," I said. I signed the paper and she took the carbon that had been attached to it and gave it to me.

"Aren't you on the basketball team?" she asked.

"Yeah."

"Good luck Wednesday," she said. "I heard that Pepperdine has a great team."

"We'll do our best," I said. I tried to sound casual. Outside I sat on the steps of the building and looked over the paper I had just signed. It was a request for discontinuation of a course or courses. The math teacher's name was signed on the bottom, granting permission. That brought me down to twelve credits. I was getting four credits in physical education, three in psychology, three in American history, and two in athletics. That left me with just two real classes.

It got me down. Because I wanted to think about myself going to school for more than basketball. I also figured that if something happened and I wasn't on the team, I would be down to six credits.

The whole thing was jive. I looked at the time, it was almost two thirty—if I had been still taking math, I would have had to hustle to get to the class. It was true, math was kicking my butt, but I didn't want to say the fight was over. Not yet, anyway. I went back to Orly Hall and stretched out across the bed. I felt like I needed a drink. Since I had been in college I hadn't had a thing to drink, not even a glass of wine, but I felt like I needed it now.

I fell asleep and didn't wake up until Sly shook me for dinner. I didn't feel like eating. I was hungry, but I didn't feel like eating, or anything. Sly said that they were going to have a poker game in the room and asked me if I wanted to play. He knew I didn't want to play. I didn't particularly like it when he was having the games, either. A bunch of guys sitting up all night smoking so many cigarettes the whole room would smell for a week.

I told Sly I was going to get something to eat. I thought about taking a walk, maybe checking out a flick. My mind flipped over to Sherry and I thought about calling her, then changed my mind. I wasn't in a good enough mood to deal with anybody.

Sometimes they had free movies at the Forum, which was like a little theater near the School of Liberal Arts. When the flicks were not free it was when they had some kind of foreign flick showing and half the people in the theater would be professors. Juice said they called them art films to let everybody know from the get-go that they weren't supposed to understand them. Sometimes they would have rock concerts on film, then it would be pretty nice. When they had the Police the whole audience got into it and started dancing in the aisles. It was pretty hip. When I checked the schedule they were having a documentary, which didn't interest me. I looked at the bulletin board on the first floor, looking for something to do, when I saw a notice for ballplayers.

The Milan Panteras, an Italian professional basketball team, will be holding tryouts for basketball players at the YMCA in Muncie on Saturday, December 2nd.

A lot of guys who couldn't make the National Basketball Association in the States went to Europe and tried out for teams there. The money wasn't as good as it was in the States, but it was still professional basketball. I thought about it and wondered if I would have a chance to make a team. The way things were going, my college career didn't look that bright. I checked the date again and told myself that maybe I'd check it out just to see what the tryouts were like. Then I went off campus to a flick.

They had this double feature. One was about an American werewolf in London. That was out-and-out disgusting. The other was about a European werewolf in New York. That was just stupid.

Pepperdine College came in the following week. They had the best-looking cheerleaders we had seen yet. Each one of their girls was a star! We couldn't keep our eyes off of them during the warm-ups.

Teufel said that Pepperdine used to have a dynamite team but they weren't doing too well the last couple of years.

"They're trying to make a comeback. They got a big boy named Purdy in the middle and this kid Hunter, who's as good as any guard in our league," Teufel said. "According to the scouting report Hunter shoots from outside and drives well, too. What we want to do is to take away his outside shot and make him do his scoring on the inside. That way they'll either have to keep their big man off the boards to make room for him or take a chance of jamming the lane. Mac, play this guy tight outside, make him go past you if he can. Wortham, Dr. Bond did the scouting report and he said Purdy got called for four three-second violations in his last game. That means he likes to stand around and wait for the ball to come to him. You make him work. If he's that lazy and still gets his points, it means he knows what to do with the ball once he does get it. Now, let's go out there and play some ball.''

We got the ball on the tap and Hauser fed Larson, who made a head fake like he was going inside and then pulled up for a short jumper. We were up by two. Larson got the ball again after Wortham had rebounded and fed Neil, cutting off Wortham. We were up by four. Then everything went wrong. Larson picked up two quick fouls and this guard that coach Teufel was talking about was eating McKinney up. Teufel switched Hauser to Hunter but Hauser couldn't do nothing with him, either. We started falling behind. Mac was off, so the only game we had was on the inside. Wortham wasn't doing much with his man, either. He was holding their center, who played a little like Go-Go, only he wasn't as good as Go-Go. He didn't have Go-Go's moves but he was bulkier and as strong as skunk pee.

Mac got a finger in his eye and the ref called time out. I thought sure I was in, but Teufel told me to sit down. Now, the way I figured, I was the only guard we had that could hold Hunter. The brother was sweet, but he was also one of them cornbread dudes with muscles in his neck, along the side of his head, everywhere. The dude would twitch his nose and the muscles alongside his head would pop up. He was sweating, stinking, and even grunting a little. But the coach in Skiptunis instead of me. Skipper was a Catholic boy from Altoona, Pennsylvania. He was one of those guys that whatever you told him to do, he'd go in and try to do it just the way you told him. Teufel told him something and he ran out onto the floor.

We had the ball, and wherever Skipper with his skinny behind and acne went, the cornbread brother would follow him. Soon as Skipper got his hands on the ball, bam! Hunter took it away, drove all the way down court, and slammed it in backwards. When they brought the ball down, Larson switched over to Hunter, leaving nobody on his man. The ball went over to Larson's man, Wortham jumped over at him, and then I heard this scream.

I looked over to where the scream came from and the cornbread brother was on the floor holding his neck. The referee called a time out but he didn't call a foul. They scored, then we scored, then they brought the ball down again.

The same thing happened, Larson left his man, Wortham switched to Larson's man, and Hauser just stood there and waved his hand. I didn't watch all the way, but I did turn back to Hunter just as Skipper elbowed him in the back of his head about as hard as I had ever seen anybody elbow a guy.

The ref called the foul on Skipper, and Hunter made a shot from the foul line, then missed the second shot but they got the rebound. This time Hunter got the ball at the top of the key. Skipper backed off and let Hunter drive down the lane. Wortham, Skipper, and Larson came over and took a shot at the brother. He fell to the ground and they called another foul on Skipper. Hunter had a bloody nose and they took him out of the game. Teufel had what he wanted. Then he took Skipper out of the game and put Mac back in.

In the second half we went ahead, and even when Hunter got in again, there wasn't too much Pepperdine could do about it. He was backing off and they didn't give him much support. They made a little flurry at the end but we still won by five points. I didn't get into the game at all.

After the game I asked Neil how come the refs let us get away with roughing the cornbread brother up like that.

" 'Cause he doesn't have any press," Neil said. "And his coach doesn't have any. If he had a name or his coach had a name, we couldn't do it. That's the way it is."

I hadn't thought much about the differences between playing ball in Harlem and playing for Montclare. Leeds had said that there was a big difference, and suddenly I was beginning to see it. In Harlem you had to be good, you had to be able to stand up and grab your space, because there was always somebody trying to grab it from you. You made a move to the hoop you had to do it strong, because there was always a brother there waiting to stop you if you were weak. But anybody could make a move. When you got the ball you did what you could do.

At Montclare it was different. There were players who could bend the rules enough to get an edge even against a better player. There were players who could put the ball on the floor a split second after they had moved their pivot foot and it wouldn't be called a violation. There were people who you could beat on, and some you couldn't touch. But when they got to the pro leagues the only name was money and you had to play street ball again, you had to be good. That's why the college teams were full of players that won trophies and went on to sell insurance while the pro teams looked like street ball all over again. Still, I was beginning to like Montclare. There were good things about it. You could look around at the students and you could see they expected to do something with their lives. That was a good thing to see, and I wanted to be a part of it. I wasn't, yet, but I wanted to be a part of it.

10

Eddie's mother called me at the dorm and said that Eddie's father was coming by the next day.

"Yeah?"

"He . . ." I could tell she was upset, but I didn't know what to say. "He comes by once in a while and he just . . . just badgers Eddie so. I told him that you were teaching him to play basketball."

"And now he wants to see how well Eddie plays?"

"And now he's going to play him a game to-morrow." Her voice was husky, and I figured she had been crying. "I wonder if you could come by. I mean, if you're here, Eddie will at least try."

I didn't want any part of it. Mrs. Brignole's business was her business. I didn't need the hassle. But I felt for Eddie. I remembered a time when I had been playing at Marcus Garvey Park and my father had said that he would come by. He didn't come until the game was almost over. I was standing at the foul line when he showed up. I was so scared of missing that shot that the referee had to tell me twice to shoot the ball. Then it didn't even reach the rim.

The house that Mrs. Brignole lived in was set back on a lawn that was too big for the house. It was the kind of lawn that people have more for show than for anything else. I rang the bell and Mrs. Brignole answered the door. She was smiling and told me to come in.

"Carl, this is Lonnie Jackson," she said. "Lonnie's been working with Eddie over at the clinic."

"Hi." Carl Brignole stood up and shook my hand. He was about six feet tall with gray eyes and dirty-blond hair. He was the kind of guy who shook your hand like the harder they squeezed the more man it made them. I took an instant dislike to the guy, which wasn't too hard, because I hadn't really liked him when I walked in the door.

"Heard you play ball for Montclare," he said.

"Right," I said.

"I played football for Tulane," he said. "You want a beer or something?"

"It's too early for beer," Mrs. Brignole said.

"June's got times for everything she does." Carl Brignole went to the refrigerator and took out two beers. "You want one?"

"No," I said.

"You here to coach Eddie, eh? Come on, let's see what he's learned."

I could see Eddie tighten up at once. He bit into his bottom lip and then he made a little jerking move with his hand. I got an idea.

I followed Carl Brignole through the kitchen and through sliding glass doors out to where a basket was set up over the garage door. I saw Mrs. Brignole in the mirror behind me. She had her arm around Eddie's shoulders.

"You know what," she said. "I think we should skip basketball today. Eddie hasn't been feeling too well, and—"

"Bull!" Carl Brignole picked up the basketball and bounced it. "How good does he have to feel to play one game of basketball? Come on, Eddie, let's see how much your big-time coach has taught you."

"Hey, I think you're taking advantage of Eddie," I said.

"Oh, yeah?" Eddie's father's jaw tensed and he squared his shoulders. "What makes you say that?"

"Well, if I'm going to coach Eddie, I should have an idea of how you play. Why don't you play me a game first, and then I'll know how to coach him."

He stood for a moment looking at me. Then, slowly, he lifted the can and finished his beer. Then he threw me the ball.

"Seven baskets," he said.

Seven baskets, sucker, I thought to myself. Check out how it feels.

I took the ball out, made a move by him, let him

catch up to me and then went up and dunked the ball. He took it out, tried to dribble around me, couldn't, then stopped and tried a jump shot. I didn't slap it completely away, just back where he could get it and try it again. He tried it again and I caught the ball in midair and turned and hit an easy jumper over him. He took the ball out and threw up a shot from about twenty-five feet that missed everything.

I made the next three baskets in a row. I felt good, better than I had for a while. No way he could even score on me. He couldn't dribble for two cents and kept trying impossible shots from way out. I decided that I wouldn't even let him have that. This little game was for Eddie, I said to myself.

Eddie and his mother were standing over to one side, near the house. I threw the ball to Eddie's father to take out, but instead of standing back and waiting for him, I picked him up as soon as he had the ball. He tried a ridiculous long jump shot and I went up and slapped it away. I glanced at Eddie.

There was a small move, but I saw it. It confused me. I looked into Eddie's face and it was sheer misery. I couldn't believe it. Here his father had been bullying the kid for all of these years, was ready to bully him again, and still he was rooting for him. I looked at Carl Brignole. There was desperation in his face. He needed to win. The bully didn't like being bullied. I took a deep breath and backed off. He dribbled close to the foul line and I jumped out at him, as if I were going for the ball. But instead of driving past me for the easy layup, he panicked and shot the ball. He ran for the rebound and I glanced at Eddie again. Yes, he wanted his father to win.

I let him get the rebound and go to the hoop. He made the layup. I let a jumper go off the side of my hand, and he got the rebound and scored again. I missed ⁻nother jumper intentionally, and he blew the layup. It wasn't even going to be easy to let the fool win.

I made the next basket and then let him slowly come back. The guy was huffing and puffing so hard I thought he'd have a heart attack before the game was over. But finally, after missing so many easy chances I could have puked, he finally won.

"You're not bad," he said, leaning bent over against the fence as he tried to catch his breath. "Especially for a freshman. You'll probably make first team next year."

"Thanks," I said.

June and I stood in front of the glass doors and watched the game between Eddie and his father.

"I don't believe he's actually giving him a chance," she said. "I really don't believe it."

"Maybe he's just changing," I said, knowing darn well that Eddie's father would probably never change.

The game was supposed to be the first seven baskets. Eddie played hard and his father let him make the game close, but he made sure that his son didn't beat him.

Afterwards we sat around and Eddie's father told me how wonderful he was at Tulane and how all the scouts had asked him to have an operation on his knee so that he could play in the National Football League.

"The way I figured," he said, "you start letting them cut on you and they never stop. I know some guys were cut open two or three times and today they can hardly walk. You see I still have good legs, good and strong."

"Yeah, right."

I hung out with the Brignoles until close to one o'clock and then I told them that I had to split. Carl Brignole walked me to the front door. He said that he was glad that I was coaching Eddie because he could see a little improvement.

"I'll be around this way in the fall again," he said. "Maybe we can get together for a beer."

I told him I'd be looking forward to it.

That Saturday we didn't have a game or practice. I told myself that I was just going to the Italian team tryouts to see what they were like. But I took my sneakers and some practice shorts that I had in the room. I took the bus to Muncie and then I took a cab to the Y where they were holding the tryouts. It was like a circus or something. It looked like anybody that had a pair of sneakers showed up. A good half of the guys were black. Some were young, some were old. One guy was about six nine. He had gray in his beard and he was losing his hair in the back of his head.

You had to sign a sheet, saying how old you were, who you had played for, that kind of thing. They also asked if you spoke Italian. I hung around where they were signing up for a while, and then I went up in the stands without putting my name down. I wouldn't have used my right name, anyway. If you tried out for a

pro team, you lost your amateur standing and couldn't
play for a college.

I saw Ray once I had reached the spot in the stands
where I wanted to be. He had on gray cutoffs and a
sweat shirt. There were a lot of guys on the floor,
maybe fifty or sixty, trying to warm up. The guys that
were running the show were Americans, not Italians,
as I thought they would be.

When everyone had been signed up, they an-
nounced that there were sixty-eight players altogether. They were going to have a game and put people in and take them out as the game went along.

The game started out with guys I had never seen or
heard of. They each had a number that they wore and
went out on the floor as the guy running the show
called the number.

"Teddy Liston, Muncie Junior College, Danny
Moses, Our Lady of the Mysteries College, Jack
Lapham, Carroll Street Devils . . ."

It went on like that, with the guys who weren't being
called giving a hand to the guys about to play. When
they got ten guys on the court they just let them play.
It was pitiful. There wasn't any coaching, and so guys
just ran up and down the court, all trying to impress
whoever was watching with what they could do. One
guy was screaming for the ball at the top of the key and
they didn't seem to want to pass the ball to him. He got
into an argument with his own team guy when the ball
was turned over. It was funny in a way; in another way,
it was pathetic. Then when they brought the ball back
down he got the ball and heaved up a shot from far
enough away to need radar. The only thing the ball

touched was the top of the backboard before it hit the clock on the wall.

I looked down at the table where the guys running the tryouts were sitting to see if they were laughing or anything. They weren't. They weren't even paying attention to what was going on out on the floor. Then I saw Sweetman.

Earl "Sweetman" Jones had been a professional basketball legend for nearly ten years. It was said, when he was playing, that he had more moves than a crab in a hot skillet. He was so bad that one of the guys who used to sing with The Miracles had written a theme song for him and they used to play it whenever he pulled one of his cool moves. He was also one of the black ballplayers that would give a hand to a young ballplayer. When I had been ready to give up on my game, it was Sweetman who convinced me that I was feeling sorry for myself, that I wasn't taking charge of my game or my life. It had hurt when he laid it on me, but it was true.

I went on down to where he was and hoped that he would remember me.

"Hey, yeah, I remember you," he said. "You trying out for this Italian team?"

"No, man, you got to be kidding," I said. "I'm playing for Montclare and I didn't have anything to do today so I thought I'd come over, maybe pick up a game later."

"How you doing at Montclare?" he asked. "You starting?"

"No, they got these white boys starting," I said. "You know how that is."

"Yeah, I know how that is." Sweetman looked at me, smiling. "Them white boys out here can play some ball, can't they?"

I had to admit that the guys on my team were good. Sweetman asked me if I was shocked to see how good they were.

"You mean the white boys?"

"I mean everybody playing on a college level," he said.

"Yeah," I said. "I guess so."

"I'm here to check on this brother," Sweetman said. "He was let go by the Nets early last year and my team needs a big forward."

"You going to give him some play?"

"I'm just here to see if he can play on his bad leg," Sweetman said. "He tore his knees up something terrible last year. The doctors figured he couldn't play anymore so they cut him loose."

"Most of these guys won't make the Italian team," I said as I watched a fat boy hit a two-handed set shot.

"They're only interested in looking at two guys," Sweetman said. "They asked them to come out and everything else is public relations."

"No lie?"

"Hey, do the Sweetman lie?"

"Who they interested in?" I asked.

"This guy Jenkins I was telling you about," Sweetman said, "and another big boy out of Bradley. They got a lot of guys over in Italy around six feet, six feet two and they can only have four Americans on the team. So the only thing they're interested in is size."

I thought about Ray. Ray was a good six five, maybe

six six, but he played smaller. He was strong but he really couldn't leap.

I watched the rest of the tryout with Sweetman. He was goofing on the players and I goofed along with him, but it wasn't that funny to me, not really.

When Jenkins got out on the floor, he played good for about five minutes. Then he grabbed his knee. He stayed out on the floor and just about took over the boards when he was out there, but you could tell his knee wasn't up to no whole lot of pounding up and down the floor.

"What you think?" I asked Sweetman.

"No way," Sweetman said. "He can't make it. Too bad he can't talk a little better. Maybe he could get into some public relations or something. Look, I'll check you out later. Glad to hear you doing okay."

Sweetman went over to the guys at the table and shook hands all around as he got ready to leave.

"Say, you know, you want to get rid of some extra tickets to any games you play against the Pacers, I'll take them off your hands," I said when he came over to shake my hand.

"You sound different than when you were up in Harlem," he said, reaching into his inside coat pocket and coming up with some tickets. "The midwesterners are teaching you how to talk like them."

"You just don't remember how I talk," I said.

"You probably don't remember either," Sweetman said.

He waved and started out, stopping to shake hands here and there and sign a few autographs. I felt good talking to him like that. I also felt good because I had decided to wait for a while before I signed up for the tryouts.

The rest of the games were about the same. There were a few names that I had heard of, guys who had played college ball and then disappeared and a few who had played some in the pros. When Ray got on the floor he was on with some real scrubs. There was no way he was going to look good with those guys. I checked out the guys at the table. They were passing around the coffee and talking among themselves. On the floor Ray was sweating hard, working hard trying to make an impression. Over on the far side of the gym a white guy stood next to a girl holding a baby. She was rubbing the back of his arm. He was going to be on the floor next. I had this feeling that he didn't have a chance to make it, and that all three of us knew it.

It was late when I got back to Montclare. I looked around for someone to go get something to eat with but everybody I knew was out. Sometimes Colin went to church on Saturday nights and I figured him to be there. Juice and Sly had probably found a party. I went over to where Go-Go and Skipper roomed. Skipper could always be counted on if you wanted someone to go eat with. He was as skinny as you could get but he was always eating. I found Go-Go but Skipper was out.

"He went to the movies with his old lady," Go-Go said.

"How she look?" I asked.

"She ain't that bad," Go-Go said. "And I think her favorite pastime is parking."

"How come guys like Skipper always find the right chicks?" I asked.

Go-Go shrugged and went back to reading his book. I wouldn't have minded rapping with him for a while, but he was one of those heavy dudes who was probably going to be a senator or something. I copped a handful of fig newtons from him and split.

I hit the bed and must have dozed right off. The next thing I knew, somebody was shaking me by the shoulder. I looked up to see Colin. He was talking on the phone and he was real white.

"Yeah, he's here now," Colin said.

"Who is it?" I asked, trying to figure out from the way Colin looked what was wrong.

"It's the campus security office," Colin said. "Ray York's dead."

"What?" I couldn't believe it.

"They wanted to know if he had any friends on campus," Colin said. "I said that we were."

We got dressed without speaking to each other. I felt confused, like somebody had made a mistake and I was part of it. I looked at the clock and it was four o'clock in the morning.

On the way over to the security office I had to stop twice because I couldn't breathe. I couldn't believe what they were saying. I had just seen him, running up and down the basketball court, his sweat shirt dark from where he was sweating, getting up for rebounds in a crowd of bodies. Now they were saying he was dead.

In the security office there were some policemen talking to Andy, the head of campus security.

"Give me your full names, fellows," Andy said, "for the record."

"Colin Young."

"Lonnie Jackson."

"Colin and Lonnie are both on the varsity basketball team," Andy said. "Ray was on the team a few years ago. Real good ballplayer."

"You guys want coffee or anything?" The policeman didn't look any older than me and Colin.

"Unh-uh." Colin shook his head. "What happened?"

"From what we can tell," the other policeman, a big, broad-shouldered guy, said, "it looks like he took his own life."

"Oh, man." I felt tears coming up inside of me and I didn't want to cry. I hadn't even known Ray that well, and I didn't know why I felt so bad, but I felt terrible. "Oh, man."

I felt somebody put a chair behind me and I sat down. I put my head down for a moment and tried to pull myself together. I put my hand over my face and took a deep breath and then I was just about together.

"What we thought"—the policeman knelt by my side—"was that, seeing how his . . . wife is all alone, maybe somebody could go by and, you know, let her talk for a bit. Sometimes that helps."

"I'll give you a lift over if you guys want to go," Andy said. "You don't have to, you know."

"We'll go," Colin said.

We got out to Ray's house and there were more police drinking coffee in the kitchen. I imagined Ray sitting at that same table, thinking about the tryouts for the Italian team, wondering if he was going to make it. Through the door I could see into the bedroom. There was a girl sitting on the bed. She had her legs crossed and one hand was in her hair. She was rocking on the bed. There was a crib and I could see a leg. The girl was either light-skinned black or white, I couldn't tell.

"Had an old piece of gun"—the policeman that was talking had big hands, the kind that could have been a carpenter's—"and he just stuck it in his mouth and pulled the trigger. Had to do it twice. She said she heard a noise that sounded like a little pop and a grunt. Said she called to him and he told her to go back to bed, then she heard another pop and he fell off the chair. Damn, you have to be a hell of a man to shoot yourself twice like that."

"Knew an old boy up near Gary," a man in civilian clothes with a police badge on his shirt pocket said through thin lips, "tried to blow his head off with an under-and-over Marlin. One of them adjustable-barrel numbers. First shell went through his cheek. He had to get up and go out to the garage to get another shell. Well, it was one cold son-of-a-bitching day and he went out there and couldn't get the lock to the garage open because the son of a bitch had frozen. He come in and called the hospital and they called us. Me and Jack Sucrette—you know Jack?"

"Goes fishing all the time? Retired last year?"

"Yeah, that's him. Me and Jack Sucrette go in and see how he's messed up. Now, we got there first before the ambulance. And old Jack, he says to this fellow, 'You want us to try to stop the bleeding or you just want to borrow another shotgun shell?' Well, that fellow got mad enough at Jack that if he had a shell he would have shot Jack."

I walked into the bedroom. I saw the kid lying in the crib. He was too big for the crib, really. The girl looked up at me and I kneeled down near her. She wasn't white, but damn close to it.

"I'm sorry," I said.

"Thank you," she said. She looked at me. Even though I was kneeling I was just as high as she was and our faces were close. Her lips were quivering and she wanted to cry.

"You want me to close the door?" I asked.

"No," she said, rocking back and forth. "I'll wait till they're gone. I'm used to waiting on things. You a friend of Ray's?"

"Yeah."

"He didn't have many friends," she said. "Sometimes he went out drinking with the guys from the mill, but they weren't really what you would call close friends."

A guy came in with a piece of paper for Ray's wife to sign. He told her that if she would just sign it where he pointed, the police would leave. She took it and the pen he pushed in front of her. By this time Colin had come in, and he took the paper from her and looked at it before she could sign it.

"Who're you?" the guy with the paper asked.

"A friend," Colin said firmly. Then he gave her the paper and told her it was all right to sign it. I wished I had done that.

She signed it, Alethea York, and gave it back to the

guy. He left, and one of the policemen came in and said that if she needed anything she could give them a call. He sounded like he meant it.

"You have anything to eat, ma'am?" Colin asked. "I could make you some eggs or something."

"I'll make something for you," she said.

"I'm not hungry," I said.

"No, neither am I," Colin said.

"Please?" she looked at us both. Then she went into the kitchen and we followed her.

We sat where the police had been sitting before. There were cigarette butts in the ashtray. She picked up the coffeepot and shook it. There was still coffee in it and she put it back on. It was the electric kind of pot. When she plugged it in there was a small orange light that glowed.

"You're not from the mill, I can tell," Alethea said. "You're too young. You from the school?"

"We play ball for the school," I said.

"We used to play ball for the school, too," she said. "I used to play on the girls' team and you know about Ray. He could never give that up, you know."

"Yes, ma'am."

"How you like your eggs?"

"Any way," I said. Colin didn't answer.

She started making the eggs. I looked over at Colin but he was looking down.

"He came home last night and he was really down," she said. "I knew he was down and it surprised me because when he left in the morning he just said he was going to some tryouts just to play a little ball and maybe we'd get a babysitter and go to the movies tonight. He wanted to see something—I forgot what it was."

She finished scrambling the eggs and put them on plates. There was another pot on the stove and she opened it and took out some sliced ham and served that.

"He was just so down when he came home. I asked him what was wrong and he said that the guys he was playing with couldn't play very well. He said something like that. I really wasn't listening that close because as soon as I heard it was about basketball . . ."

We ate the eggs and some ham and had the coffee black. She had only coffee and sat at the end of the table. She was crying but she wasn't making any noise. Her eyes were gray, and they were filling up with tears that spilled over her thin cheeks. She was thin, but she could have been pretty if she fixed herself up a little. Sometimes she would look up and catch me and Colin looking at her and try to force a smile.

"He always felt he was too close to making it to just give up," she said. "He always said it was an inch higher, a half-step faster, one more shot, between the guys that made it and the ones that didn't. He was working on his outside shot. Sometimes, when he wasn't hitting it, he would come home and just sit by himself in the bedroom. He wouldn't want to have anything to do with me or Jimmy."

"That's your son?"

She nodded.

"The police said that if you needed anything . . ." Colin said. "But you could call us . . ."

"I'm going to wait here a few days and then maybe

I'll go to St. Louis," Alethea said. "I've got some people there. I've got a teacher's license. You know, he made me go back to school after the baby was born and get my teacher's license?"

"That was a good idea," Colin said.

"I'll probaby go to St. Louis because I've got people there," she went on. "I got people in Oklahoma, too, but I didn't fulfill their dreams. I was supposed to go to college and be a teacher."

"You can still be a teacher," I said.

"I know, but I just don't want them to be thinking that I'm okay now that . . ."

We talked for a while longer; then the police came by again and asked some more questions. A guy from the school paper came and got some details about what Ray had been doing. A minister and his wife came by and said that they were going to stay with Alethea for a while and Colin and I said that we would be back and to call us if she needed anything.

"I just want to say again that I'm sorry," I said.

"It's okay." Alethea took my hand. "He just put so much into it and when nothing worked out for him, I mean with the basketball and everything, he just took it so hard. I thought he was going to be okay because he knew that he couldn't make the Italian team when he went to the tryouts, but when he came back he was still . . ."

Colin was almost out the door when I stopped to look at Alethea York.

"Don't worry about me," she said. "I'll get along. And thanks for coming by."

"He had a chance to make the team," I said. "He

played okay, except that the guys he was playing with just weren't that good, so it made him look bad."

"No, they were only there to look at two players," she said. "Ray knew one of the organizers and called him before the tryouts. He said he just went for the game."

"Oh," I said.

"Did you go with him?" she asked.

"Yeah."

We got outside and the car from the campus was still there and the guy took us back to Orly. I felt like nothing. I kept remembering Ray playing at the try-outs, running up and down the courts hustling every minute. What the hell had he been hustling for? They weren't keeping score and he knew he didn't have a chance to make the team. What the hell had he been hustling for?

We got back to Orly Hall and to the room and both of us flopped across our beds. For a long time I just lay there, not really thinking even, or maybe thinking so many scattered thoughts that none of them made sense.

"Hey, Lonnie?" Colin called to me.

"What?"

"You okay, man?"

"Yeah."

"I didn't know you were that close to Ray," he said. "I just figured that if they were calling around looking for a friend, it wouldn't cost us too much to be friends. You know what I mean?"

"Yeah. Hey, can I tell you something?"

"Go ahead."

"You know, I wasn't that close to Ray," I said. "I mean, I'm sorry he's dead and everything, I really am, but I wasn't that close to him. But when they told me that he was dead, and then that he killed himself . . ."

"You feel like it could have been you?"

"Something like that."

"Lonnie?"

"Yeah?"

"I felt a little like that myself. Sometimes this whole college thing seems so strange to me. I'm supposed to think that I'll be a big-time ballplayer, or at least finish school. There's only one thing that makes it even possible to believe any of it."

"What's that?"

"I don't have anything else to believe in."

Ray's family came and they decided to take him home to Chicago to bury him. They had a little service for him in a chapel in town and a few people showed up. The only ones from the team were me, Larson, and Colin. We said good-bye to Alethea and she asked if we would mind if she wrote to us. I said no, but I didn't know why she would want to write. I think it had something to do with Ray being a ballplayer and us being ballplayers and her not wanting to just throw it all away so soon. I think Ray would have understood that too.

The day after the service Skipper sprained his ankle at practice and Teufel told me that I'd be the third guard when we played Gary that weekend.

"Maybe we'll swing you back and forth between

guard and forward," he said. "That could work out fine if Wortham's not up to it."

They ran a lot of plays for Go-Go to practice. They ran them against Wortham and Go-Go looked okay, but he still wasn't Wortham. Wortham was a monster at practice. He knew that they were getting Go-Go ready to replace him and he showed everybody—Teufel, Leeds, and Go-Go—that he was still the man.

Larson and Hauser caught up with me after practice and started rapping as we left the gym. Once in a while I rapped to Larson, but I almost never spoke to Hauser.

"You hear how Hauser gets his speed?" Larson asked.

"How's that?" I asked, looking at Hauser.

"Larson is so full of crap that it's coming out his ears," Hauser said. "Don't listen to him, bright eyes, he'll rot your mind."

"He gets McKinney to pour wintergreen up his butt and it has a jet effect."

"One time I twisted my back," Hauser said, "and the trainer was away for the weekend. We were just practicing. So I told Mac to put some oil of wintergreen on my back. Instead of that he just pours it on my rear end—and you know where it goes—"

"He took off around the gym like a thoroughbred," Larson said.

"Hey, look, bright eyes," Hauser said. "If you get a lot of time against Gary, you might play against Bradley, too. Skipper's ankle looks like it'll be hurt for a while. And if you play back court against Bradley, we'll have to work something out. We'll have to talk about it when you have a chance. Okay?"

"Yeah," I said, wondering what he meant.

"Look, I'll see you at practice tomorrow." Hauser waved and veered off toward the science building.

"What was all that about?" I asked Larson after Hauser had left.

"There's a guy on Bradley's squad that a lot of the pros are looking at," Larson said. "He's only about an inch bigger than Hauser. If Hauser has a big game against this guy, then he might get a tumble from the pros. If he has a bad game against this guy, he can forget it."

"So he needs me to help him look good," I said.

"One hand washes the other."

"Yeah."

"Look, the Fat Man wants to see you," Larson said.

"About what?"

"I don't know, he didn't tell me," Larson said. "You afraid of the Fat Man? You sound afraid."

"Yeah, maybe I am," I said.

"That figures," Larson said. "But if you get up any nerve, why don't you give him a call?"

I couldn't get to sleep. I kept thinking about Ray and what must have gone through his mind at the Panteras tryouts. What must have happened, I thought, was that even though he knew what the deal was, that they weren't looking for players other than the ones they had already been scouting, Ray must have figured he had some kind of outside shot of them signing him. What had made me feel so bad when I heard about Ray doing himself in was that deep in my heart I knew that all I had was an outside shot, too. I wasn't bringing much to Montclare that anybody seemed to want. Sometimes I felt like just packing my stuff and going back to Harlem.

But there were times I didn't want to leave. There were times, on the basketball court, when I knew how Ray must have felt. There were moments when I would be on the floor and the ball would come to me and the world would be round and pebble-grained and in the palm of my hand. Other dudes would be around me, trying to get the ball, trying to snatch my play away, but they couldn't. Suddenly I would feel full of power and full of life. There was no place on earth other than the court where I had ever felt that, and the moments were like some kind of crazy magic that was happening to me.

Maybe some of them bright guys who turned out to be doctors could go into an operating room and look at a person lying on an operating table and feel the same way, I don't know. But for guys like me, and Ray, it was different. On the court, once we got the ball we knew we could do it. Muscle and drive and quickness gave everything in life a meaning.

Anyplace else we wouldn't even get the ball.

Montclare was not the world I knew, and I felt that it wasn't the world I belonged to, either. But I knew it was a world that had some things in it that I wanted, and that I had a slim chance of making it after all. I told myself that I wasn't ever going to give up. I wasn't going to shoot myself, or run away, or let anybody push me out. If I had an outside shot, I was going to take it.

I was tired the next morning when Larson came around and said the Fat Man was dying to see me. He ran down this stuff about how the Fat Man only wanted to talk to me for a few minutes and that I should just drop by and talk to him.

"What he want to talk to me about?" I asked.

"Look, the Fat Man has been a good friend to me for a long time," Larson said. "I'm not going to start questioning him on everything he says. The guy's been cool with me, so I'll be cool with him."

I told Larson I'd think about it.

The classes eased off a bit. That is, they were still hard but I didn't go into a panic thing anymore. At first, when I was in history class and the professor would ask a question, I'd look the other way and hope he wouldn't call on me. But after a while I didn't tighten up if he called on me and at least I could try to figure out what he was talking about. A lot of the other kids put their answers a lot better than I could, but I was beginning to understand the stuff as well as most of them. I could see that a lot of them would be trying to jive the professor with answers that didn't say anything and he would call them down for it.

But if the classes were easing off, my thing with Sherry was beginning to get me a little uptight. Back in Harlem I had always had some kind of woman. In Montclare the closest thing I had was Sherry, and I wasn't really getting next to her. The thing was, I figured, there must have been a difference between middle-class chicks and the way they operated and the kinds of chicks I used to know. If a chick got up in your face with a lot of grinning and conversation, it meant that she was interested in you, and if she started throwing some heavy kisses and things your way, it meant she was looking for you to be her man or at least get into some kind of heavy action. That wasn't what was going down with me and Sherry.

Sherry would flash that nice smile, get your heart beating kind of fast, then throw a few soul kisses on you and walk away while you stood there with your motor running. Then she would come back with some talk about not being ready for no "serious" commitment. If I had been in the streets I probably would have just said later, but Montclare only had a handful of black chicks at best and Sherry, at least, would talk to you. Still, I couldn't understand where she was coming from. Once I saw her and Linda, her white roomie, in the rec room and I wondered if Sherry was AC-DC. They were holding hands when I walked into the room and then Linda gave her a little hug and split. I told her that I didn't know that she and Linda were "that" kind of roomies and Sherry blew up. We were still in the rec room and she threw a bag of potato chips at me and ran upstairs crying.

I went up to her room thinking that if she was crying she'd probably be there. Then I thought that if Linda was there, she might be with her. I didn't want no big confrontation thing but I didn't want it to ride, either So many people were getting messed around so bad, it seemed, and I didn't want to be part of the people who messed the others up.

I knocked on the door and there wasn't any answer. I tried the door and it was open, so I just walked in. Linda was out and Sherry was lying on the bed. I went over to her and sat next to her on the bed. She looked up and saw it was me and turned away.

"I'm sorry," I said.

She had the sheet twisted around her arm and her face was tucked under her hand so that she looked like a bird putting its head under its wing. She didn't answer me and I just sat next to her. There wasn't no whole lot I could say—I had put my mouth on the girl already and didn't have no place to back out to. We sat like that for a good half hour before she moved. I thought she had fallen asleep. She got up and went to the bathroom and then came out and sat next to me on the bed.

"You want to go get something to eat?" I asked.

"Not hungry."

"I'm real sorry about what I said, you know. I like you a lot, but I really don't know how—I've never met anybody like you before so I don't know how to deal with you. I met some—what you call yourself? middle-class? upper-class?—girls before but they were real la-de-da, you know, like they were something more than me. You don't act like that, but then you don't act like anything else I know, either. I guess when I saw you and Linda together this morning I was maybe—what? —looking for an excuse why I couldn't connect with you or something."

"And now?"

"Now it don't matter if I connect with you or not," I said. "You still okay and we can be friends if you want."

"Do you want to be friends?"

"Yeah, look, I can use some friends out here," I said.

"But you still think I might be making it with Linda?" Sherry asked.

"It don't make a difference, is what I'm trying to say," I said. "We can be friends on any level you want."

"Are you and Colin making it?"

"You know better than that, baby," I said. "That's so ridiculous I won't even get mad."

"But if I go and spend the weekend with Linda or hang around her, I have to be making it with her, right?"

"Okay, what was all that about this morning?"

"It was about me really being down," Sherry said. "It was about me being out here in Indiana without many friends and about Linda being here from California without many friends. That's what it was all about.

"Back home I didn't have that many friends, but I had a few good buddies, you know?"

"Yeah?"

"Well, most of them went to college, but I was the only one to come to Indiana." Sherry moved back on the bed and folded her legs in front of her, Indian fashion. She had a birthmark on her right thigh. "When I got out here I found that there weren't many black students. At first it didn't bother me because I get along with the white kids as well as I get along with anyone else. Then I thought about dating and I saw that practically the only black guys out here were the guys on the teams. Half of them aren't worth two cents and the others just expect me to say hello and start undressing. I dated a few white boys but I wasn't too comfortable doing that."

"You did?" I said. "I didn't know that."

"That was the whole point. I didn't want anyone to know," Sherry said. "You want a Coke?"

"Yeah, okay."

I watched as she went to her drawer, got some change, and then went into the hall. I was surprised that Sherry was having any trouble at all in school, because she looked really cool all the time. I was also surprised that she had dated white guys. She came back with two Cokes and handed me one before she got back into her squat-legged position on the bed.

"Anyway—"

"You were talking about dating white guys," I reminded her.

"Yes. Well, I kind of arranged the dates so that not too many people would know about them. I'd tell them I had to buy some new sneakers or a new wrist band and that they should meet me at the sports store."

"So you could meet them off campus."

"Right. And I liked some of the guys but I wasn't comfortable. Some of them wanted to hit on me right away, too. I was trying to make up my mind about you, I guess."

"So what about me, you finish making up your mind yet?"

"No, but I got all the ifs and ands put together. You want to hear 'em?"

"Yeah, go ahead."

"On one hand you seem like a pretty nice guy . . .

sometimes," Sherry said. She had put her Coke down and I could see she had really been doing some thinking about the whole thing. "You're nice-looking, you have a nice body—"

"True, true."

It made me feel good to see her smile.

"Most of all you seem interested in my track, which is what I'm about. That's your big plus. You seem interested in what I'm about."

"Which means?"

"Which means that you've got me in a state of culture shock," she said. "Then there's the one plus one theory that my mother has."

"What's that?"

"She says you have to look out when you only find one guy around that you like. You start adding things up and your one and his one make an easy two."

"Sounds right to me," I said. I had tried to sit squat-legged like she was, but it hurt my knees too much and I straightened out my legs.

"One plus one equals that *particular* two," Sherry said. "But if there's a lot of guys around that you like, or could like, you look for the best because none of them is the only thing around. Dig it?"

"Well, where does that put me and you?" I asked.

"You mean what should we do?"

"Yeah?"

"What you should do is to worship the ground I walk on and be faithful and true to me and never look at another girl and every night you can go to sleep and dream lustful thoughts about me," Sherry said. She was laughing.

"And what you going to be doing?" I asked.

"I don't know," she said. She stood up and went over to the door. "But if you can catch me you can find out."

"How am I supposed to catch you and you're a track star?" I asked.

"You mean, I'm not worth the effort?"

I stood up but my heart wasn't in it. The chick was turning me on again and she knew it. She also knew that by the time I got across the room she could be halfway down the hall. I started to jump, hoping I could surprise her and freeze her for a moment before she could take off. Instead I stumbled and fell across the floor. I was pissed. I was just in front of her feet. I looked up to see Sherry smiling.

"Oh," she said, reaching over and turning off the light switch near the door. "You got me."

I stood slowly and took her into my arms. I kissed her forehead, then lifted her chin gently until our lips met. She clung to me tightly as I kissed her again and again.

"There's a French restaurant just off campus if you want to get a bite to eat," she murmured. "Maybe we can get the last bus if it hasn't gone yet."

"If it has," I said, "you can just hop on my back and we'll fly."

The way I felt right then I could have, too.

11

The next day I decided to go see what the Fat Man wanted. I didn't think anything was wrong with it, but I decided against wearing the school sweater.

I had never seen the Fat Man working in his pizza place before. Most of the time he just sat around and read the papers or added up columns of numbers on the backs of envelopes. This time he was kneading the dough. His huge hands looked as if he were strangling it. The white dough came through his fingers as he squeezed it, then he would pat it into a round ball, only to start strangling it again.

"Lonnie, you know I do a lot of betting," he said,

not looking at me. "I enjoy it. I don't make any money at it, but I enjoy it. You know what I mean?"

"Yeah."

"Yeah, sure you do.

"Now, I talked to Larson. That Larson, he's a class ballplayer. I don't know if he's a class guy, but he's a class ballplayer. I tell him that to his face. I mean, I got nothing to lose by telling people what I think of them. Anyways, I talked to him and I asked him to do me a favor. I asked him to beat this Gary Tech team you're going to be playing this weekend good. You know, run up the score. Sometimes you play against a team of rinky-dinks and you play just enough to win. So I say to him, Larson, the heck with it, run it up. Some clown comes along and he likes this team and wants to lay down a bet with me, that's his business. Only he ain't stupid. Some people are weak, mind you, but ain't nobody stupid."

The dough was in a round ball and the Fat Man started slapping it flat with the palm of his hands.

"So the guy ain't stupid, so he's going to take his team with the points. I give him ten points and he figures maybe his team won't win but they'll come within ten points. You know what I mean?"

"Yeah." I nodded.

"Yeah, yeah, sure. But if you guys play like you know how this team won't get within twenty points of you. I'm so sure you're gonna win big, I'm gonna put a hundred and fifty bucks extra down on the game for you."

"For me?"

"I know you don't need the money," the Fat Man

said. "You play ball because you're getting an education. That's the way it's supposed to be. You win big and I'll consider it a personal favor, because that's what it will be.

"Hey, you see what I'm making? It ain't pizza. I'm beating it up too much for pizza. It's what they call pan bread. You make a stew on top of it and you bake the whole thing. I can't eat pizza, I got a bad gut. I swear to God, I got a bad gut."

Gary Tech was unbeaten and the townie paper, *The Dispatch*, said that we were to be their first major test. A local cable company carried the game as their Wednesday Sports Special. They did a long interview before the game on their center. He was close to seven feet tall and had huge hands. We were favored to win by ten points but Larson told me that the spread had been bet down to seven points. Their forwards were six six and six seven and it didn't look good for us. Bobby had liquor on his breath before the game and Hauser noticed it and said something to Leeds. Leeds made Bobby wash his mouth out with Scope. I guess that was how they dealt with his alcohol problem.

I couldn't see how we were even going to stay with this team, let alone beat them. That is, I couldn't until the game started. We got the tap. Hauser brought the ball down and passed to Neil in the corner, who scored. Then they started bringing the ball down but Hauser stole the ball at midcourt and took it in by himself and we were up by four. They brought the ball down again and this time Hauser and Mac trapped their guard, who threw it back court so we got the ball again. They didn't have a guard on their team worth two cents. Their big man looked good, but they couldn't get the ball up court to give him a chance at it.

Larson played like a madman for the whole first half, and by the time the half ended, we were up by fifteen points. It looked like a runaway.

In the locker room Teufel ate a cheese sandwich and Leeds went over who he was going to put in for the second half. I heard him telling Skipper and Go-Go that they would be playing the second half. Larson went up to him and talked into his ear and then Leeds went over and talked to Teufel. I didn't know what was going on but I remembered what the Fat Man had said about running up the score.

The second half started with Go-Go, me, Larson, Hauser, and Mac on the floor. We played run-and-shoot ball like we were out in the playground or something. Their team was good when they got the ball in deep, but we didn't let them get it in deep. When Larson wasn't in the game, he kept yelling from the sidelines for us to "work." We ran the score up pretty good before Teufel took Hauser and Mac out and put in Skipper and Sly. Sly was quick, even quicker than Hauser, and he stole the ball the first time he went after it. If he could have shot from the outside the way Hauser did, he would have been a great ballplayer. The way it was, though, he would get the open shot but still look to pass off. Hauser had scored sixteen points in the first half and seven in the second before he left. Sly only scored one point, on a free throw, but his game wasn't that bad.

Juice didn't get much play, but he did get in. Their

big man gave Go-Go all he could handle and then some. We won the game ninety-two to sixty-four.

Back at Orly Hall I was lying on the bed and staring up at the ceiling while I listened to Sly and Juice lie about how many chicks they had gone to bed with, when the phone rang.

"That's probably one of my women now," Juice said.

Colin got the phone and said it was for me. It was the Fat Man saying that he was just calling to tell me I had a nice game.

"Who was it?" Sly asked when I'd hung up. "The White House?"

"The White House?"

"When I have a nice game, the Prez usually calls me from the White House and congratulates me," Sly said. "He used to let his old lady do it, but then he got suspicious because she stayed on the phone so long."

"Just some dude I met in town talking about how good a game I got," I said.

Juice and Sly went back to their lying and I lay back down on the bed, but my hands were sweating. I asked myself, if I wasn't doing anything wrong, how come my hands were sweating?

The Fat Man had said to run the score up and we had, but the whole team was part of it, not just me. Even Teufel and Leeds acted as if they didn't mind us running up the score.

"I got this chick," Juice said, "who's so desperate for my body that I got to keep an extra set of buttons with me when I go to see her because she tears them off getting at my clothes."

"That ain't nothing," Sly said. "I got these two twins, they're nurses. While one is loving me to death, the other one is giving me mouth-to-mouth resuscitation so I don't die completely and ruin her chance."

I took another shower to get away from Sly and Juice. I thought about Sherry and decided to call her when I finished. I had some money, close to thirty dollars, but I had to buy my meal tickets and pay my laundry bill. I figured out how much that would be, and that I would have about three dollars left. I thought about the money the Fat Man had talked about. I could have used it, I thought, but I wasn't going to take it.

When I got out of the shower, I called Sherry. She said she was going to be busy.

"What are you going to be doing?" I asked, more to have something to say than anything else.

"Why?"

"Is it a secret?"

"No," Sherry said.

"So?"

"So what?"

"So what are you going to be doing?"

There was a long pause on the other end as I waited for Sherry to say something. I was sitting on Colin's bed. He was sitting near the window shining his shoes. From where I was sitting I could see something sticking out from under my pillow.

"I'm going out with a guy I used to date," Sherry said.

"Hey, there's nothing wrong with that," I said. "You make it sound like a big deal."

"Wow, you're really okay," Sherry said. "I really thought you'd go into a big thing about Bill."

"Bill?"

"Bill Williams," Sherry said. "His mother belongs to the same sorority that my mother belongs to, that kind of thing. He asked me last week if I would go out with him and I didn't know that . . . you know."

"Yeah, no big thing," I said. "Have a nice time. Maybe I'll see you tomorrow."

"Sure."

I let her hang up the phone and then I slammed the receiver down. I was really steamed. I felt like running up to Sherry's room and going upside her head.

"What's the matter?" Colin asked.

"You know Sherry, right?"

"Yeah, that's that fine black girl who's got your head facing in the wrong direction."

"She ain't got my head facing in no wrong direction," I said. "She's just a jive chickie I'm thinking about getting next to."

"That's why you slammed the phone down?" Colin looked up at me, then down at the shoe between his legs. He started buffing the shoe carefully with a shine rag. "Everybody is impressed by Sherry. She was here during the summer taking a few credits. Larson tried to hit on her, a couple of guys from the football team, they all made a play."

"Yeah?"

"And they all went away saying she wasn't anything because they couldn't get to first base. Everybody knows you dated her."

"Yeah, but now she's supposed to be going out with somebody who asked her for a date a week ago."

"You and her something special now?"

"Told you she wasn't nothing special," I said.

"Because I'm just waiting for the right time to make my move," Colin said.

"Lame as you are?" I said. "You don't stand a chance."

"Well, you didn't make it," Colin said.

"No, but we got this understanding, see . . ."

"You, Sherry, and this guy she's going out with?"

"Shut up, man." I threw Juice's pillow at Colin and he ducked it easily.

"I'm going out with this waitress in town," Colin said, slipping into his shoes.

"She good-looking?"

"Nope."

"She got money?"

"Nope."

"What she got, a nice personality?"

"Nope."

"Then why you going out with her?"

"She brings the Danish," Colin said.

I lay down on my bed and watched Colin laughing at me. He checked his watch, gave me the "thumbs up" sign, and split.

When he had left I looked under the pillow and got the envelope. I opened it and saw three new fifty-dollar bills. I figured the Fat Man must had given it to Larson to put there. I took a deep breath and pushed the money back up under the pillow.

My stomach started cramping and I had to go to the

bathroom. I sat on the john a while and I noticed that my hands were sweating. I tried to think of what the Fat Man had said to me about betting on the game, and doing him a personal favor. I thought about it until my head began to ache. Then I began to check myself out. Here I was, sweating bullets in a john thousands of miles from home trying to figure out if I was cool or if I wasn't. I didn't need this mess. I didn't need it at all.

I got myself together and decided I was going to burn the money. I went and locked the door and looked around for some matches. I was still scared. I didn't have any matches and I looked into Colin's drawer. He had some matches. As I reached for them I noticed something else. It was the announcement for the service they held for Ray. There was an address at the bottom, and I knew it was where his wife was staying.

I took an envelope that didn't have the school's name printed on it, addressed it, put a piece of plain paper around the fifty-dollar bills, and sealed them in the envelope. I bought a stamp from a machine on the first floor and took the envelope all the way across campus to mail.

12

"Eddie's mother called," Ann said. "It seems that Eddie's father was paying for his sessions here. Now he doesn't want Eddie coming here anymore."

"How come?"

"Because he came over to the center last week and saw some of the handicapped children playing in the gym. He said that he doesn't want his child treated as some kind of 'freak.' "

"You go along with that?" I asked.

"No, but more important, the doctors said that he's shown the first real progress in years since he's been working with you. You've been the only thing that brings him out of his shell."

"What his mama say?"

"She agrees with us, she wants him to come, but Eddie . . ."

"He don't want to do nothing against what his father says, right?"

"You got it."

"Crap!"

"It doesn't mean that you're out of a job," Ann said. "You can keep coming over and help keep the equipment in order. And you can always work out with me. I could use some mat work."

"I bet you could," I said, "but right now I've got to figure out something for Eddie."

I had a half an idea which I wasn't sure would work and I started out the door when Ann called me back. I turned to see what she wanted and saw her sitting on the desk, legs crossed.

"Don't forget me," she said, smiling.

"I won't," I said.

Mrs. Brignole was playing cards with friends when I reached the house. They looked at me as if they weren't sure if they should put their hands up or make a break for the door.

"Oh, hello, Lonnie." She got up and started to introduce me to the other women around the small bridge table. They forced smiles to their faces which died quickly as I nodded to each. I saw Eddie through the doorway sitting in the next room. He was sitting in a chair facing the window, slowly rocking. "What . . . what can I do for you? I guess you've been to the center?"

"I was having a little trouble with my jump shot," I

said. "I thought that since Eddie has seen it a lot, maybe he would go with me out back and watch me shoot it a few times to see if he could see what I was doing wrong?"

She took a deep breath, smoothed her dress down in front of her, and then walked into the room where Eddie still sat. I followed her.

"Eddie, Lonnie has been having a little trouble with his . . . with *what?*"

"My jump shot," I said.

"Right, his jump shot. And he wonders if he went out back if you would watch him shoot it and see what he was doing wrong."

Eddie didn't answer. Then he shrugged one shoulder. He shrugged it again and then looked up at me. There was a smile. Not a big one, but just a little smile. The cat was glad to see me.

He got up and walked out to the backyard.

"Lonnie," June Brignole whispered to me. "I can't pay you."

"You know anything about math?"

"I used to teach it," she said. "If you need help . . ."

"Maybe we can talk about it later," I said. I went out back with Eddie and we began playing. I thought about his mother helping with me my math. In a way, I didn't want her or anyone else to know how much help I needed, but in another way it was a big relief. If I was going to stay at Montclare, I had to get on with filling in some gaps. Math would be as good a place as any to start.

Teufel put us through twice-a-day practices for the next week. One practice we would run through plays and the other we would scrimmage and have pass drills. They were hard, but I worked them with everything I had. What I was thinking was that I wanted another year at Montclare. I think the shock of the place was wearing off a little and I wanted to take another look at it.

One day we stopped practice so a photographer could take pictures of all the players. First they took a team picture, then they took pictures of the guys in a light scrimmage, and finally they posed each of the guys. They had me standing on a high stool with the ball over the basket like I was just about ready to dunk. Then they had me posing as if I was dribbling, only they had a special ball with tape on it that I could put my finger through and hold it still so the picture wouldn't blur. They said that they were going to hand out the pictures to the press. Teufel told the photographer not to give us copies, because it might go to our heads. Then he had us run laps around the gym.

I met Sly after practice. His moms had sent him a record player, and I helped him carry it up to the room. He put on a side and I fell across the bed. I was feeling cool and looking at the schedule, trying to figure out how many games we could win and what tournaments we might get into after the season when Colin came in. He had a container of coffee with him. When he saw me on the bed he put his fingers on his lips and beckoned for me to come with him. I thought he was up to something, because he was a real clown. It was kind of funny, because he looked so serious, yet he would get in on any joke we pulled. He didn't say a word until we got out into the hallway.

"C'mon, man, let's take a walk," he said.

"What's up?"

"Let's walk for a while first."

He was looking serious and I figured it probably wasn't a joke but I wasn't a hundred percent. We went out of Orly Hall and across the grounds until we reached Monument Field, where they held parades for the ROTC and things like that.

"What's up?" I asked.

"Two guys came over to me and started asking me questions about fixing games," Colin said. "They asked me if I had heard any rumors about games being fixed or points being shaved."

"When did this happen?" I asked.

"About two days ago," Colin said. "They asked a lot of questions about you, too."

"Me? Like what?"

"Did you spend a lot of money, did you fly home much, that kind of thing," Colin said. "I saw them talking to Teufel. Leeds, too."

"Nobody talked to me about anything," I said.

"The way they were asking the questions," Colin said, "they seemed to be fishing around."

"Wait a minute." We were in the middle of the field. "Who are you talking about?"

"I don't know who these guys were," Colin said. He took his glasses off and wiped them off on his shirt. "At first they came up to me and started asking me stuff like what the point spread was for the game we have this weekend. I told them I didn't know. Then they told me that I did know. 'You're playing in the game and you don't even know the point spread?' this guy says to me. So I told him to go take a walk. Then Leeds comes up to me and tells me to tell these guys anything I know. They asked me if I had heard anybody talking about the point spread. Did I see anything funny going on in the games? Did I know some guy called the Fat Man? I said I didn't.

"Then they started asking me questions about you. How much money you had. Did you use drugs, that kind of thing. I told him that you didn't use anything, you were usually broke. Then they told me not to talk to you or anybody about the conversation. I've been imagining they've bugged everything from the gym to my jock shorts. I swear to God, it scared the hell out of me. I don't think anybody's shaving points in our games. I told them that. Then they asked me why we ran the score up in the last game. It was a regular third degree."

Panic. My testicles shriveled up into a tight little knot and my stomach did flip-flops. All the while Colin was talking to me the only thing I could do was to listen for my name. I couldn't even make sense out of what he was saying.

I told him there wasn't anything to it, that it was just a routine thing they probably did. But it bothered me a lot that they had talked to Colin and hadn't talked to me. It bothered me even more that they had talked to Leeds.

I thought about the hundred and fifty bucks that had been under the pillow. It came to me that maybe the Fat Man hadn't left it, that the investigators had.

"Lonnie, if you're involved in anything and you need my help—" Colin looked at me.

"I'm not involved in anything," I said. "But you know, it's strange stuff."

"You can say that again." Colin shook his head. "I know I haven't done anything and they made me so nervous I wanted to confess. For a while there I didn't know what to do."

Neither did I. I went over everything that had happened again and again. I knew I hadn't shaved any points, but I did help run the score up and I had taken some money from the Fat Man for the mill game.

I went back to the cafeteria with Colin and we had greasy hamburgers and half-cooked french fries. We were supposed to have a practice the next day, a day off, and then the game on Saturday. Later, I went through my wallet until I found what I was looking for, a small piece of lined paper with a telephone number on it. I dialed it with my right hand while I kept the fingers of my left hand crossed. A woman's voice answered the phone and I explained to her who I was. She told me to hang on for a moment. It seemed longer than any moment but then a deep voice spoke into the receiver. It was Sweetman.

He listened to what I had to say and then asked me if I knew where the Holiday Inn was in Indianapolis. I didn't know but I figured I could find it.

"The Brotherhood is supposed to be meeting in Cleveland tomorrow," Sweetman said, "but I'll just switch the meeting to Indianapolis. You be there at three and ask for me."

"What's the Brotherhood?" I asked.

"Be there if you're serious," Sweetman said. "And you'll find out."

There was a click and I held on to the phone for another minute before I realized that Sweetman had hung up. I didn't know what was going on, or what the Brotherhood was, but I was going to find out.

I got the bus to Indianapolis the first thing in the morning. I knew I was going to miss the last practice before the game but I also knew I could be in big trouble. I told Colin to tell Teufel that I had an upset stomach.

I found the Holiday Inn in Indianapolis and asked the clerk for Sweetman.

"You a ballplayer, too?" The clerk was a young guy but his hair was just about snow-white.

"Yeah," I said.

He gave me a room number and I went up and knocked on the door. Sweetman opened it. He was dressed in a pair of white slacks and a white silk shirt that was open at the collar. He was wearing gold chains around his neck the way he always had, but now there was some gray in the hairs on his chest.

"Hey, what's happening?" I said.

"Look." Sweetman stopped me by putting his hand against my chest. "You gave me a story about somebody investigating a point-shaving bit. I heard you and you're here. Here's what the deal is. I'm going to walk into that room over there and close the door. You think about this for a minute or two and you think about it strong.

"Now, if you shaved any points, just one, what you do is turn around and walk out of here, because I ain't got no use for you. If you wrong, you just wrong, brother. Don't lie to me and don't lie to the Brotherhood. Because if you lie to us, we're going to see that you get messed up because you're messing with the one thing we got going for us and that's our integrity. You think about what you've done, and what you haven't done. If you did what the man said, walk on out of here and nobody knows you were even here. If you clean, brother, and I mean *squeaky* clean, come on in that door."

Sweetman turned and walked through the door he had pointed to and closed it behind him.

The dude shook me. I didn't know what to do. I took a deep breath and held it for a minute. I hadn't shaved any points, not even one. I had never played a game that I hadn't done my best. I took another breath and went into the room.

The room was small. There was a bed, a table, a television, and a telephone. There were a few cans of beer lying around and some glasses. Sweetman was there and four other ballplayers. Sweetman pointed to a chair and I went to it and sat down.

"Don't start into no light rap," one brother said, "because this ain't no social visit. Everything you tell Sweetman is true?"

"Yes it is," I said.

"This Fat Man dude, he didn't tell you to keep the score down in any games?" I recognized the toughest defensive guard in the NBA.

"No, he didn't say nothing about any of the games we played," I said. " 'Cept, you know . . ."

"You know *what?*" It was Rashid Abdul, the premier center for nine years, speaking.

"The last game, he said he didn't like the other team and we should really put it to them."

"Run the score up?" Sweetman said.

"Just . . . yeah, I guess so."

"Setting up the spread," Rashid said. "You beat that team by a lot and he gets a break on the spread in the next game. Instead of you being a four-point favorite you got a rep for scoring a lot of points so now you're a six-point favorite, maybe even seven. Now all he got to do is to keep the score within three or four points and he's got it made."

"I ain't doing nothing like that," I said.

"Don't have to," Sweetman said. "If the word gets out that it's done, you'll be the first one they suspect, especially since you already been fool enough to be around the dude. You knew Cal Jones, didn't you? Cal didn't tell you to watch out for dudes like this Fat Man?"

"He said to watch out for guys trying to get me to fix games," I said.

"They probably won't try to fix it if the word is out." It was another brother, Jumping Joe Biggs, stretched out on the bed. "They probably gonna lay cool for a while."

"Maybe not," Rashid said. "They might not know about it, because Sweetman says they didn't talk to Lonnie and maybe they didn't talk to whoever else is in on the deal. You remember back when they thought something funny was going on up in Boston, they didn't talk to nobody except that one white dude?"

"Yeah."

"Then they came down on everybody. 'Nother thing, they may try to set the brother up to take a fall if it looks a little shaky."

"Who introduced you to this Fat Man?" Sweetman asked.

"Guy from the team," I said. "His name is Larson."

"Play forward?"

"Yeah."

"He got a nice game," Rashid said. "Auerbach was looking at him."

"Auerbach looking at all the white boys who can play," Sweetman said. "But he's the guy Lonnie's got to watch."

"Yeah, and stay away from the Fat Man," Sweetman said.

"I'm going to tell him that I don't want nothing to do with him," I said.

"Hey, what did Sweetman say?" Biggs got up on one elbow. "He say 'Go tell Fat Man this'? No! He say 'Go tell Fat Man that'? No! He said to keep your black butt away from the Fat Man!"

"If he call you up and say he got to see you, just hang up the phone. Don't say nothing to him," Sweetman said.

"And you got to check out the game when you play," Biggs went on. "There's two ways they can fix a game. They can play around with the ball at the end of the game, throw it away a few times, but that's hard. Or they can play around with it at the beginning of the second half. You favored to win this game by how many points?"

"I don't know," I said.

"Look in the paper, Sweetman." Rashid pointed to a paper on the small table.

Sweetman picked the paper up and turned to the sports section and looked up our game.

"The gambling line is five," Sweetman said. "You supposed to win by five points."

"They got that right in the papers?" I asked.

"They put it in the papers so the bookies and the fixers know what they got to deal with," Rashid said. "Then the papers are the first one hollering if somebody wants to shave points."

"Okay," Biggs went on. "You favored to win by five, so that means it's going to be a pretty close game, but it ain't that close. A real close game you can throw the ball away at the end and keep the score where you want it. You start talking about five points and you need to get your team behind sometime so you can catch up at the end. If your team is behind and you work hard to catch up, it don't look like you're shaving points because everybody sees how hard you working in the end. They don't notice that when the game just started you threw away five or ten points to get yourself in that position."

"Yeah, you got to watch out for the first part of the game," Sweetman said. "If the game is going to get funny, that's where it's going to have to be. Your team falls behind and then everybody hustling to catch up. And if it's an easy game, the passes start going to you at funny times and you all of a sudden's the one that missing the ball."

"Cats be shaking their heads at you like you doing something wrong."

"What they saying, young brother"—the guard looked me up and down—"is that you got to make sure the team plays together in the first half, don't let the team fall behind. Then if somebody wants to pull some mess they got to come out in the open with it. You dig?"

"Yeah," I said.

"We gonna have some of our people watching your next game," Sweetman said. "If there's any funny stuff, we'll know it just as fast as everybody else, faster. We can pull some coats that you can't pull."

"I really appreciate this," I said. "I was really worried for a while."

"You ain't out the woods yet," Rashid said. "So stay worried."

"And we ain't doing it just for you," Sweetman said. "Every brother that's out there playing gets jived around when one brother blows. You know that. Now, why don't you get on back to campus."

"Hey, I really thank you guys," I said. "You taking time out to—"

"We don't want your conversation," Rashid said. "You really ain't got that much to say."

"Huh? Yeah, well, okay." I started out the door.

"Yo, brother!" Biggs called me back.

"I just wanted to tell you that not only is your conversation light, your game ain't much either!"

They all cracked on that, like they had made some big joke. I got a little pissed and walked on out. I didn't think they had to crack on me like that. But I was glad there was a Brotherhood.

We had to get to the gym an hour before the game. We went through our warm-up drills and everybody was loose. I looked around the stadium to see if I could spot anybody from the Brotherhood but the only black faces I saw were students. It made me a little nervous, but I figured maybe something would happen by the time the game got going.

"What we're going to do," Teufel said, "is to give them their outside shooting, and take away their inside game. That's our defensive style. They usually have a good balance of outside shooting and layups. But they don't have that strong a rebounding team. Most teams that play them worry too much about their outside shooting. No team is going to beat you without an inside game. We've got to work on position from the time the game starts until you hear the buzzer."

Teufel went from man to man, patting us on the shoulders and telling us to relax. Franklin was the second toughest conference team we were supposed to face, and if we could beat these guys, we'd only have to worry about Wichita State.

Bobby started at center and controlled the tip to Hauser. We got the ball, brought it down, and couldn't get a shot off for a good thirty seconds. When we did get it off, it was a jumper by Bobby from the foul line which rolled around the rim twice before falling in. For some reason I thought we would control the game from the outset, but it was all sweat and struggle. We were falling behind, but nobody was screwing up. They were just all over us. Hauser hit a few shots from

the outside and Bobby got a tap in and made two foul
shots early but we were quickly behind, twenty to
twelve.

They were playing us as close as I could imagine
anybody playing. The brother holding me was short
but quick and kept slapping my wrists going for the
ball, but the ref wouldn't call it. Teufel called some set
plays, but even they didn't work and we were free-
lancing all over the place. We played tight defense,
too, which kept us in the game, but barely.

Everything that Sweetman and the others had said
about the game getting away from us in the first part
was coming true, but it looked as if they were just a
better team than we were. At least it did in a way, but
in another way it didn't. They were playing fairly good
defense but individually it looked like we should be
able to take them. When I got the ball, the only shots
I'd had were from twenty feet or more. I thought of
going one on one—even though I knew Teufel didn't
like it. But I also thought I had to do something to get
us back in the game, the way the Brotherhood had
said. Then I realized what was going on.

Hauser was bringing the ball down with me. Neil
was being covered by a pretty quick dude who kept
him outside. Hauser's man was playing him close, too
close, but Hauser was looking to pass. Wortham was
being double-teamed, which left one man open, Larson. At least it should have left one man open, but
Larson never turned toward the ball. Either that or he
went into the low post with Wortham when the middle
was already jammed up. He was taking himself out of
the game. I got the ball at the high post from Wortham

and put it on the floor. He moved away from me and Larson went with him. I took my man to the hoop and scored. But I knew I couldn't do it all by myself. Larson, by his keeping away from the ball, gave us a four-man offense to their five-man defense.

We scored as Wortham hit a hook. When they inbounded the ball, I went for the steal and fouled a guy. I held my hand up as the ref pointed at me. Their forward missed the foul shot, we rebounded, and Neil hit on a short jumper at the buzzer ending the first half. I felt sick to my stomach. I glanced up at the scoreboard as we walked off the court. We were down by eleven, forty-nine to thirty-eight. We could make it up if things went right for us. If we all busted our chops; if Larson played like an All-American.

"Wortham, what the hell are you doing out there?" Leeds was red and the veins in his neck stuck out. "You look like you're sleepwalking! If you don't get some movement in the center, nothing's gonna work!"

Teufel went over some plays, talking about overloading one side of the zone as if we didn't know how to do that. He told Wortham that the game was in his hands. That all he had to do was to wake up and play up to his capability.

"If you want us to, we'll start Go-Go," Leeds said.

"Bobby will be okay in the second half," Teufel said. "Won't you, Bobby?"

Bobby nodded his head. I knew what the scenario was. We would all go out and bust our tails in the second half, Larson would put on a big show, and the All-American would win the game.

We went out for the second half. I didn't feel like

much, didn't feel like anything really. I looked around the stands at a sea of white faces looking down at me, and the only thing I could think of was that I was going to screw up.

We got the tap and Larson went in and made a three-point play. He looked good, putting a move on their center to make the point and draw the foul. Bobby hit a soft jumper and we were only behind by six. I thought back to what the Brotherhood had said. Don't let a fixer hide, make him come out into the open. He has to fix the points in the beginning of the period or come out. Larson had made his show basket, and was going to start hiding again until it was time for us to take away the game. Maybe, I thought, maybe not.

I didn't like Hauser. I thought he was just like every other redneck I had met. He didn't make any bones about not liking me, either. But I knew he wanted to win. I knew he wanted to win as badly as he wanted to breathe.

"Let's overplay their guards," I said as we came back down court on defense together. "If they get by us, let's let our All-Americans handle them."

"Stop thinking, bright eyes," Hauser said without looking at me. "It'll give you a headache."

I felt like taking a swing at him, but all of a sudden he was gone. He took a chance, gambled that their guard wasn't alert, and went after the ball. I trailed him down court but I didn't need to, he made an easy layup. They brought the ball down again, I went after it, missed it, and scrambled back. I faked going after the ball again, didn't go, and their guard threw it away. Hauser got it and we were down by one.

Wortham began to control the defensive boards. They had one shot at their basket and that was it. In a matter of minutes we were up by five instead of being down.

The game settled down, they sent in another forward, a guy who could handle the ball and help out in bringing it down. Me and Hauser backed off the steals and just tried to contain them. Wortham got hot and we were up by ten.

Hauser tipped a pass to Larson, who led the break. Their guards scrambled after him but they wouldn't have caught him. He passed anyway—at the feet of a surprised Hauser. The ball went out of bounds. Come on out, Mr. Larson.

"Okay, settle it down," Larson said. We were at the bench. I was wiping the perspiration from my neck and face. "All we have to do is to play it cool and we've got these guys. Concentrate on the ball."

I wasn't sure what was happening or how it was happening, but we got into the same kind of game that we were in at the beginning. Only now we were calling it ball control and they were creeping up. Franklin got within one point when Larson snatched a rebound, took it all the way down the floor himself, and shot the softest jumper I had ever seen in my life. It didn't touch anything but net. We were up by three. Larson picked off another pass with seconds to go, dribbled around until he was fouled, then made the first and missed the second. We won the game, under five points.

The game was over and some of the cheerleaders were congratulating Larson. Some guys from the school's television channel were waiting to interview him. In the locker room I asked Skipper how many points Larson had scored.

"Sixteen," Skipper said. "He was high man on the team. And five rebounds. You had nine points and five rebounds."

Was I wrong? Was the game straight all the way? I didn't know. I thought it over, but I wasn't sure. I knew that at the end of the game it had been Larson who had iced it for us.

Colin had played for a few minutes and had scored three points and pulled down two rebounds. He had also made two fouls. I was thinking about getting on his case for that as I left the gym. My foot was sore. I hadn't noticed it during the game. I thought about going back to the training room and having a look at it, but decided not to bother. It was a crisp, cool night, and I just wanted to get back to Orly Hall.

"Hey, Jackson, nice game." A short guy with a lot of teeth came up to me. "We're lucky to have you out there with Mac hurt."

"I hope I can get some playing time when he comes back," I said.

"I think Teufel will probably go to using three guards," the short guy said. "Hauser's a junior and McKinney's a senior. He's got to get somebody else ready."

"Yeah, probably," I said, feeling pretty good. I enjoyed talking with the guy. There were some chicks up ahead of us and I felt like running after them and

talking with them about the game, too. Winning made
you feel good.

"Say, I saw the Fat Man," the short guy said. "He
said to tell you you played a nice game. Maybe you can
drop around the pizza shop tomorrow."

"Oh, yeah?"

"Yeah, and he said to give him a call tonight."

"I got nothing to talk to him about," I said, "or you
either. Why don't you just split."

"Don't get touchy," Shorty said. "I don't care if you
call him or not, or if you pick up your money."

"I don't know what you're talking about," I said,
trying my best to breathe normally.

"Oh, well, maybe you better come with me anyway."

He stepped in front of me and held up his hand. In
the middle of his palm was a badge.

I went with the guy to the administration building.
Teufel was there and Leeds. They asked me if I knew
the Fat Man. I said yes. Then they asked me if he had
ever given me or offered me money to change the
outcome of a game. I said no. Then they told me that I
was suspended from the team until they made an investigation.

I couldn't do anything for the whole week. I
couldn't go to class, I couldn't eat, nothing. It wasn't
that I was sick or anything, it was just that every bit of
energy was drained from me. The first day or so I just
sat in the room. Then my roomies started getting on
my case, trying to cheer me up and whatnot, and I just
couldn't take that.

I had some money and so I went to town and sat in
La Hispania and drank beer. I figured they would kick

me off the team even though I really hadn't done anything wrong. I remembered the article that Cal had shown me, it seemed a thousand years ago now, about how he had been put out of the NBA for associating with criminals, something like that.

I went back to the dorm at night for the first few days, waiting until it was late so I wouldn't have to talk to the others. One night Colin was awake when I got in.

"Lonnie?"

"Yeah."

"Lonnie, if you need somebody to pray with, or get drunk with," Colin said, "I'm here."

"Okay, farm boy."

I got my money from the hospital center and went on a real tear. I just drank till the money ran out, and by the weekend I was in La Hispania trying to bum drinks from people I didn't even know.

"Hi, you stand a little company?"

Sherry eased into the seat opposite me.

"What are you doing here?" My voice sounded like tires over a gravel driveway. "I thought nice girls like you didn't belong in places like this."

"Could be," Sherry said. "But I heard that nice guys like you don't belong in places like this, either. That's why I looked everywhere else in the world for you before I came here. Colin finally found you here yesterday."

"Colin? Here?"

"He thought you might not remember him being here," Sherry said. "He told me he wasn't sure whether to just sit in here with you or knock you out and take you back to the dorm. He's been sitting here."

I looked over to where Sherry was pointing and saw Colin seated at a table near the wall.

"Who told him to come here?" I said.

"I don't know why he came here," Sherry said. "But it really puzzles me why he stays. They say you called him a lot of racial names, the whole bit. You even took a swing at him."

"Crap."

"Lonnie, my roomie is away playing tennis this week. Why don't you come and stay with me? They've extended your suspension for three days. Come on with me."

"So you can feel sorry for me? Look, I don't need that garbage. All I need is some dust to get me back to Harlem."

"That really what you need?"

"That's it."

"You spend the three days with me," Sherry said. "Just until the suspension ends, and I'll give you the money to get back to Harlem. Square business?"

"You got the money?"

"I can get it from my folks."

"Bet."

I thought spending three days with Sherry was going to be a problem. It wasn't my first problem. Standing up was my first problem. My head was pounding and I had more aches than I had places to keep them. Colin came over when he saw I was getting ready to leave. He tried to help me but I pushed him away. I wasn't mad at him, not really, but being mad was the only thing I had at the time. We got a cab outside La Hispania and went back to the dorm. There were some stares in the lobby, and I stared back.

I felt dirty, and out of place and small. I let Sherry and Colin help me up to her room and fell across the bed.

When I woke up it was dark. I could smell food, but I couldn't remember where I was. I tried to get up and my head started swimming again.

"Lonnie?"

It was Sherry's voice and I remembered where I was. She switched on the light. There were french fries and a cheeseburger on the table between the two beds. She must have brought them for me but couldn't get me up. I got up and stumbled past her to the bathroom. I felt better after coming out of the bathroom, but when Sherry saw me she winced. She got a towel out of one of the drawers and handed it to me.

It was probably the first time I had had my clothes off that week. In the shower the hot water was running over my body and felt good, even when it found the small scrapes I had accumulated. It revived me somewhat. I dried off, rinsed my mouth out with some Listerine that Sherry had, and came out of the bathroom feeling halfway decent again.

"You look vaguely human," she said. "Nothing to brag about, I mean, but vaguely human."

I got back into her roomie's bed and tried to think of something to say to this middle-class black girl. I didn't know anything more about middle-class black people than I did about white people. I had put her into a category, had framed and labeled her, and she was coming out of a different bag altogether. I got myself up on one elbow to say something, but she just put her fingers to her lips and shut out the light.

When I woke in the morning it was just in time to dash out of bed and into the john, where I puked my guts. I threw up until I was weak. Sherry was there with a towel and helped me clean myself. I felt dizzy and ashamed of myself. I saw some of my clothes neatly folded on a chair, and started to put them on. Sherry stopped me.

"Baby, don't," she said. "Just lie down until you feel better. That's all you have to do."

"You feeling like a mama today?" I asked.

She nodded. "I guess so," she said. "I feel like taking care of you. You'll be all right soon. Maybe even tonight. Just let yourself relax for a few more hours."

I got back in the bed and let Sherry pull the covers over me. She let me rest for a while and then got some toast and eggs from the cafeteria. I managed to deal with the toast, but just barely. Then she asked if I minded if she read to me.

"I have to read this book for English lit anyway," she said. "They're short pieces by Larry Melford. This first story is called 'The Meetings.'"

She began to read. Her voice was clear and warm and I could tell she was enjoying the story. I was enjoying it, too. But more than that, I was enjoying Sherry. I had been feeling sorry for myself, and I still was. But no matter how things turned out at Montclare I had done some cool things and met some cool people. Colin was one of them, and Sherry was something else again.

I drifted off to sleep, and when I woke she was still there. The shades had been drawn and she was reading by the light from the lamp.

"Is it late?" I asked.

"No," she said. "It's a little chilly out. I thought closing the drapes would keep the room warmer."

"Oh."

She continued to read. I couldn't tell if it was the same book or not. I had lost a sense of time and I wasn't feeling well enough to concentrate on the story. But I concentrated on her voice and the fact that she was still there. I took my arm from under the cover and put it on her leg. She stopped reading and looked at me.

"Hey, girl, I think I love you," I said.

She put her head down, and when she lifted it there were tears in her eyes. "How do you expect me to read to you if you're going to get me all upset?" she said.

I kissed her hand, and she began to read again.

I must have dozed off again, because the next thing I knew Sherry was shaking me by the shoulder and calling my name. There was a phone call for me and she pushed the receiver into my hand. A voice on the other end of the line said that the investigation was over and that I should come over to the administration building at once.

I told Sherry what it was all about and she said she would come with me.

"Uh-uh," I said. "Because I'm not going."

"Why not? Don't you want to find out what happened?"

"No," I said, "I don't."

"Lonnie, are you scared?"

"Nope." I sat up and took the clothing from the chair. "I've seen a lot badder turkeys than these out here, mama."

"Then why are you putting on your bad-Harlem-cat act?" Sherry asked. "If you're not scared, why don't you go over there and face them? I think you're scared out of your mind."

"Maybe I am," I said. "I don't know."

"Lonnie, you're so good, you're really so . . . so real now."

"What are you talking about?"

"You can tell me that you're scared," she said. "That's great. You couldn't have done that when you first came here. And you said that you loved me before. You remember that? You weren't just being sick and talking out of your head, were you?"

"No, but don't talk too much about that," I said. "Because that's scarier than going to the administration building."

"Lonnie, go," Sherry said. "If it doesn't come out right, we can get a lawyer or something. We'll fight it together."

"You a fighter, too?"

"No," she said. She ran her fingertips down the side of my face. "But I think you are."

Leeds was waiting in the office talking to the secretary when I walked in. He looked at me and pointed toward one of the chairs. I went and sat in it. It was a silly thing to do, but I had to smile. The secretary picked up her phone and dialed a number. I heard her tell somebody I was there. Then she nodded and hung up the phone.

"You can go in now," she said, looking from me to Leeds.

What I wanted more than anything else was to go to the bathroom. All the courage I had gotten up when I was talking to Sherry was in the pit of my stomach waiting to slip out. I walked behind Leeds into the large office. There was one of those long desks that reflected the windows. Teufel was sitting at the desk, the president of the college, two secretaries, some guys I had never seen before, and Abdul Rashid, from the Brotherhood. I wanted to just go over and kiss him for being there.

"Lonnie, we've held a thorough investigation of some allegations that were brought before us. There were suggestions that some of the players were being tampered with. Do you have any knowledge whatsoever of anything to this effect?" the president asked.

I wasn't ready for the question. I thought of saying that I thought Larson might have been doing something, or what the Brotherhood had told me about how a game would go if someone was shaving points, but I figured that Rashid could speak on that if he wanted to, and I really wasn't sure about Larson.

"No, sir," I said.

"Mr. Leeds, you're the assistant coach, is that correct?"

"Yes, sir."

"Do you have any knowledge of any tampering with the athletes or illegal contacts?"

"No, sir, I do not."

"Well, our investigations have indicated that there has been some illegal contact. Now, this is a very unfortunate situation. However, I don't think it will affect the school in a major way. Mr. Lydell here is with the investigation unit of the state police, and he'll fill you in on the details."

"At first we heard a number of rumors." Lydell was a tall guy with a pointy head. He looked like a policeman. "We tracked down some rumors about point shaving and about fixing games. We came up with no significant findings along these lines. We did, however, discover that a certain Mr. Alfredo Corsi had talked to some of the ballplayers and that one of them for a monetary consideration signed a letter of intent to play for an Italian team."

"That letter of intent"—the president took it from there—"has effectively terminated Bill Larson's amateur status and his eligibility at Montclare. We thought for a while that Lonnie had been involved with this as well, but we're glad to find that he wasn't. So we're reinstating Lonnie on the team.

"Frankly, I don't care how much this is talked about on campus. This kind of thing does nothing but hurt the athletes, so the more it's known about, the better. Lonnie, I heard you went through some rough moments as a result of the suspension, and I'm sorry. But the fact that your name is clear is as much a relief to the school and to me personally as it must be to you."

We all shook hands, and Leeds talked about how much Larson would probably get to play with the Italian team and even some compliments about how well I was playing.

"You know that since you've missed a week of practice you're going to have to work twice as hard to catch up," Leeds said.

"Yeah," I said.

I was numb by the time I got back to the dorm. I hadn't known anything about Larson and the Italian team. I hadn't remembered him at the tryouts, just Ray.

"Hey, no-count, you buying the Cokes?" Rashid Abdul put his elbow on top of the Coke machine.

I went through my pockets and found that I didn't have a penny and told him.

"You ain't good for nothing!" Abdul said. "You ain't never gonna be a ballplayer because you're lame. How you walk around with no money in your pocket when you know I might want a Coke?"

"I was just in a—"

"Man, shut up, you ain't got nothing to say anyway," Abdul said. "What you think about that hearing?"

"I didn't know that he was thinking of going to an Italian team," I said.

"Neither did he," Abdul said. "He'll be in the NBA in a year or two."

"Wait a minute—" I said. "You mean—"

"What I mean," Abdul said, "is that they started sniffing around, and when they found where the stink was leading them, they stopped sniffing before they found the doo-doo. They came up with a reason Larson had all the money he was sporting and the case was closed. The Italian team thing was a compromise. The Italians went for it and Larson didn't have a choice. They really didn't have anything on you, and the Brotherhood was there watching so they couldn't push anything on you."

"Man, I got to thank you cats."

"There you go running your mouth again," Abdul said. "That all they teach you in this school? Here, I got something for you."

He reached into his inside coat pocket and handed me a white envelope.

"Go on, fool, open it up. It's from the Brother-hood."

I opened it and found a small metal mirror.

"What's this for?" I asked.

"That's so you can start watching your own rear end for a change." Abdul grinned. "The Brotherhood can't watch it for you all the time."

Some co-eds came over and asked Abdul for his autograph. He took out his pen and told me to get away from him because I was hurting his image. The guy was a snap.

I hurried back to the dorm to tell Sherry what had happened. She took one look at my face and figured the whole thing.

"How do you feel?" she said, smiling.

"Like half past nine on Christmas morning," I said, taking her hands in mine.

"You tell Colin yet?"

"Not yet."

"Well, let's go tell him before you start feeling too good, Mr. Lonnie Jackson."

Without Larson we lost to Rice, but it wasn't a con-ference game. Hauser said we played all right and that we'd really be tough by the time Go-Go had a little more experience.

"Teufel might even switch him to forward down the stretch," Hauser said. "With you and me in the back court and Mac coming off the bench, we'll be okay, bright eyes."

"Yeah, okay."

The next game I got seats for Eddie Brignole and

his mother. I worked my tail off and we won with Bobby scoring big from the inside. After the game we felt good in the locker room. There was a lot of kidding around, a lot of jokes. We were winners and everybody was happy. They were kidding Sly about a play that he had made. He had got the ball near the foul line and taken four steps to the basket without ever dribbling the ball and for some reason the refs didn't call it.

"The feet are quicker than the eye, especially when they belong to Sly," Sly said.

Even Teufel managed a smile. Winning covered a lot of things.

"Hey, Lonnie, there's a woman outside wants to see you," Go-Go said. "If she's got a sister, I'm available."

I thought it was Sherry, but it was June Brignole with Eddie. She wanted to thank me for the tickets. I told her it was okay and that I would bring Eddie home.

I took Eddie into the locker room and told the guys that he was a buddy of mine.

"He's helping me with my jump shot," I said.

They kidded with Eddie, and Colin found a small shirt to give him. I watched Eddie Brignole as he stood among the guys. His eyes darted around and he was as happy as I had ever seen him. It wasn't anything special, but just being one of the guys mattered to him. Maybe he had dreamt about being a ballplayer and he was edging toward that dream here in the locker room. Same as I was.

Sherry met us outside the gym, and together we

took the bus to Eddie's house. I had to carry him the two blocks from the bus because he had fallen asleep.

"I can get him upstairs," June Brignole said.

Eddie woke as I put him down, looked up at his mother, and hugged her. I said good-bye and, with my arm around Sherry, started to leave.

"Lonnie!"

I turned and saw Eddie standing in the doorway, half hidden behind his mother's dress. I went back to him and took him by the shoulders.

"Hey, my man, you'd better get some sleep if you're going to help me with my game tomorrow," I said. "I can't stand no sleepy coaching."

"Lonnie," he said, "you're a *real* nice guy."

I held him for a long while, trying to hold my tears back. Then I stood and gave him five. He yawned, and I figured he'd be asleep by the time me and Sherry got to the bus stop.

We were doing okay, me and Eddie, I thought as Sherry took my arm. It wasn't going to be easy and maybe neither of us would make it in any big way, but that's the way it was. Nothing we could do about that. But Eddie had a chance, a good chance, to live the way he'd want to live. And for the first time in my life, I felt that I did, too. And somehow it was about a lot more than playing ball. It was about knowing what was out there, what to go for, and what to walk away from. I figured Eddie to play it to the bust if he had half a chance, and so would I. That was all for the long run, though. But for then and there, we were both doing okay.